I0659652

Path of Ink

Rebecca Jayne Heipel

ISBN: 978-0-9948656-4-9

To my grandma Lavone, may you watch me write from the stars.

Prologue

The age of technology had surpassed all its creators could have ever imagined. Going above and beyond what all blockbuster movies had ever dreamed of. Everything and anything that you could desire was accessible with at the touch of a button and for the most part instantaneously. Computers became even faster and tinier until they were incorporated into wearable contact lens controlled by your thoughts. Swiftly came the day where internet accessibility was done seamlessly by your mind and holographic touch screens appeared wherever you stood. You could work from anywhere, at any time. Robots were utilized in all manners, from production in large manufacturing plants, to inside hospitals doing complex surgeries, to being play toys for the rich. If there was something you wanted and it wasn't available a simple inquiry online would make it become a reality. The world lived in an age where there were endless possibilities, endless needs, endless wants and no one to say no. It was a fast lane to paradise in the making.

But with all good things, we as a race turned a blind eye to the potential harm each advancement brought us. People lost the desire to do manual labour and those jobs were quickly turned over to the robots. Physical store fronts became obsolete and unemployment went on all time rise. People travelled less with the invention of virtual reality and human interaction begin to decline. People stopped forming relationships and the birth rate dropped drastically. Crime increased amongst those too poor to afford the newest technology as they realized that the prisons contained all the basic amenities that they could not afford. Humanity had reached a point where there was no one to teach, no one to educate, no one to further the path we no longer walked on. We were a slave to our pleasures and vices.

This continued decade upon decade. Until finally, due mostly to poor design and the belief of omnipotence, the robots began to fall apart. Fear of them surpassing us had prevented us from designing robots that could learn and fix themselves. Their intelligence had been stifled from the very beginning all because a few robots had once created a language to talk amongst themselves that we couldn't understand. As we got lazier our dependence on them grew, yet no one had thought to learn how to look after them. And like everything commercially made they weren't built to last, but to fall apart relatively quickly so consumers would be forced to buy the newest and latest model. No one noticed that at some point there weren't anymore robot designers. That the latest model was exactly the same as the last only it sported a brighter flashy new colour. They too had fallen prey to the luxuries of life.

One by one, people began to notice that their pampered lives were disintegrating. Awaking from their dreams they found that they had lost their place in society. Few had left the sanctuary of their homes in years and found themselves physically unable to do so. Food was quickly becoming scarce, water was no longer being purified and no one knew how to help themselves, let alone each other. Old governments reassembled trying to figure out what to do. But their minds had been muddled by decades of idleness and self indulgence. No one could make a choice, let alone think.

In all of the movies once made long ago, the end of humanity had always been dramatic. A plague would wipe them out, global wars with aliens wanting to inhabit their planet, the military accidentally releases chemicals that would turn us all into mindless, flesh eating zombies. Not once did anyone ever make a movie where we simply withered away. Where we would just sit and stare off into the space, wondering about what we should do next. Never, in all of humanities time had we developed into so useless a species.

Yet, there was a single ray of hope. A small group of scientists, once deemed dangerous by the government, had diligently fought against the natural urges to succumb to the pleasures of life. As the world around them isolated themselves, they gathered in small groups looking for ways to stop the devolution of life around them.

After almost fifty years of research, a group of four men had come up with a terrifying and yet brilliant solution to a problem the government had once felt impossible. A chemical that could rewire the human brain, reprogram new skillsets and reawaken motivation. They approached the government with this idea and had been met with eager hands and full wallets. Without any proper testing the government secretly implemented the scientists plan to save humanity before it was too late. They released

4

the toxin into the atmosphere and within days every single human targeted had been infected. In less than a week people were no longer sitting in their homes lost in their own little worlds. They were actively contributing to society. They became motivated to learn. To work. To exist.

As the last of the robots broke down they began to act and think for themselves once again. People began to interact with one another and the population, dangerously close to extinction, began to rebuild.

The government grateful for the sudden rebirth of humanity quickly turned its back on the scientists. They were once again shunned and deemed heretics. Their urgent warnings of the solution only being a temporary fix was disregarded. They were forced into the shadows and quickly dissolved back into their lone existence.

All except two. A Dr. Fredrickson and his assistant Charles were kept close to the government's side. Dr. Fredrickson had been the one to originally come up with the formula for the toxin. Charles had devised the planetary wide distribution device. While the other scientists fought the government, Dr. Fredrickson had turned suit and joined forces against his former colleagues. He quickly agreed to the propaganda the government volleyed and thusly gained what little funds they could to continue on their side project. Together, Dr. Fredrickson and Charles made sure the system would never stop and thus humanity would be 'saved' forever.

TWENTY YEARS LATER

Dr. Fredrickson and Charles looked at the monitor flickering in front of them. It was one of the few computers that still somewhat functioned in the world today. Computers had died off with the robots when the number of people able to build or repair dwindled with time. Only a small handful of people had the needed intelligence to keep some of the basic systems functioning properly. As of current, the primary computer system that was kept up and running efficiently were the ones needed to scan tattoos. Outside of those, only the government had computers and they were bare bone basics at that. Gone were the days of global communication at the touch of your fingertips. Back were telegram like messages sent via the few computers left.

Despite what first seemed to be a more thriving humanity, people were still dying quickly. Disease was running rampant, crime had increased and the quality of life was continuing to degrade. There were more children then there were adults. Several adults had died due to an illness brought upon by the first round of the toxin released. When they had first launched the toxin, hormones were one of the first systems affected and humans had eagerly jumped back into 'interaction' with each other. But their bodies were weak and several women died during childbirth. It took close to a decade before anyone was sufficiently trained for basic medical care and people had gained back adequate physical strength. As a result there had been a large baby boom around five years earlier. For the first time in almost a century there was abundantly more births then deaths.

The gap in age was staggering. The majority of people who had recently given birth were in their seventies and eighties. Children were being left to fend for themselves, forcing the need for a more efficient control system of the barcodes that appeared on people. Dr. Fredrickson and Charles had been working around the clock streamlining the process and expanding its original projections. What at first was a motivational guideline for how individuals would to contribute to society became a day to day decision maker. Therefore bringing humanity back to where they had originally been. They both knew that this would happen and instead of putting up a fight like the other scientists had, they gave the government exactly what they wanted. They knew that they were essentially putting humanity in yet another bubble. Another cage where there would be no escape. Not unlike the death sentence that they had only narrowly evaded. They had hoped to build a way out. A trap door, to give humanity a much needed ladder to something better. It was simply a matter of time.

They looked at each other and sighed.

"What time is it?" Dr. Fredrickson asked as he continued inputting data into the large supercomputer.

"Its almost dawn. We should return to the surface soon before the others arrive." Charles said.

Dr. Fredrickson's forehead crinkled as his nose curled up. "You stay here and finish what you're working on. I'll let you know when its safe to come up. No one will notice your absence."

Charles nodded in agreement. Dr. Fredrickson inputted the last bit of data and patted the computer fondly. He closed his eyes briefly and said a small prayer. A left over affectation from his youth. He then began the long climb up the staircase to the surface.

Charles watched as the doctor became a tiny speck in the distance until he disappeared entirely. He heard the clang and hiss of the airlock shaft far above shutting behind the doctor.

Dr. Fredrickson closed the airlock behind himself and scanned his retina to lock it. Now only he or Charles could open it. He passed thru the scaffolding in front of the entrance, lifting a work blanket out of his way that was strategically placed across the scaffolding. The door at the end of the hallway slammed open and several men quickly entered. They wore military uniforms and held theirs guns directly at him. He took a step back letting the work blanket fall back down, partially hiding him. His hand hovered over the control panel. A solider pulled the work blanket off, dust filling the air and long empty paint cans clattering to the floor.

Dr. Fredrickson examined the group calmly, "This is a restricted area. On who's authority are you here?"

The officers parted as a tall man with broad shoulders entered. The skin on his face sagged heavily, showing a man that was once severely overweight who then lost the weight from malnutrition, opposed to proper eating and exercise. An unfortunate side effect from decades of being attached to feeding machines and virtual reality devices. A common sight in todays world. His hair had regrown, but was patchy in colour. Unlike the others, he bore no barcode on his wrist. One of the few immune to the toxin, much like the doctor and the rest of the government that had originally sanctioned it.

"I did." The man stated. His chin was held higher than normal, a smirk dancing across his lips.

"Whatever for Richard? You know I have the authority and jurisdiction here." Dr. Fredrickson sighed, holding his position within the scaffolding.

"Tell me doctor, what exactly are you doing down there? What silly games are you conceling from us?" Richard said snarling.

Dr. Fredrickson held his ground, his eyes unwavering, revealing nothing. "You know very well what I'm doing down there. Improving the toxin." As he spoke he repositioned himself so that his body was physically hiding his hand behind his back. He knew that it would look like he was hiding something, but it was a risk he was willing to take.

"We all feel that the toxin is working quite

well. Why improve what is already perfect?" Richard asked him.

Dr. Fredrickson smiled. "You know as well as I, that nothing is ever perfect. Just look at yourself?" he said with a snide chuckle.

Richard immediately flushed over and began to stammer. "My physical appearance is not what is up for debate here. Your acts of treason are."

Dr. Fredrickson's eyes flickered briefly as he began to punch a sequence on the console behind him. "Treason? Me? Don't be ludicrous Richard."

"I have it on good authority, from one of your fellow scientists, that you are building something devious in secret down there." Richard said.

"Charles? Whatever could Charles have told you about? We're simply adapting the toxin to help the children who are soon to be without adult supervision. They aren't ready to survive on their own."

"Not Charles, me." A whiny and snivelling voice wafted in from behind Richard. From the shadows a short, hunched over man in a white lab coat appeared. It took Dr. Fredrickson several moments to recognize the man. Once physically as strong as he was intelligent he now was a withered old man that hobbled with a

cane.   His old partner before Charles; Dr.
Holdin.   The two of them once ran an
organization that had been disassembled by the
government years ago for their radical over the
top ideas.   He was one of the doctors that Dr.
Fredrickson had quickly tossed aside when he
and Charles had sided with the government.
His ideas, although much like Dr. Fredricksons,
had always gone in a sinister direction. Where
Dr. Fredrickson had wanted to help humanity,
Holdin wanted to control it. When the toxin had
shown signs of working Dr. Holdin had
suggested ways to adapt it to allow the
government more control over the people. Dr.
Fredrickson had quickly dismissed his partners
findings and pushed Holdin out of the picture
during negotiations with the government.
Apparently, man had never really evolved past
the desire to be 'king'. Ironically, in order to
keep the government at bay Dr. Fredrickson had
relinquished much of the toxins control to them
much as Dr. Holdin had originally predicted.

"Dr. Holdin here says that you are building
some kind of device. That the area below us is
not a research facility but an old alien space
craft. Leftover remnants from our governments
Area 51 project." Richard stated, his voice
quavering with excitement.

Dr. Fredrickson looked from Dr. Holdin to

Richard. He ascertained that neither were operating within official capacity. He hadn't seen Dr. Holdin in several years and doubted he had any relevant information to prove treason. He also knew that the officers present would kill him without hesitation. He looked at the airlock briefly, closed his eyes and prayed for forgiveness. He knew that there would be enough air in the craft below him for Charles to survive for at least few years. There was also enough rations for him to survive longer than that if need be. Hopefully Charles had set up the one way communication device at his home so he at the very least could say his goodbyes to his family. He also hoped that Charles had remembered to bring down the last set of specimens needed.

"Doctor? What have you to say?" Dr. Holdin said with a smirk.

Dr. Fredrickson smiled. "Goodbye?" he said as he punched in the final sequence in the console behind him.

The airlock squealed as air escaped out in a loud hiss. Dr. Holdin shrieked and an officer let loose a spray of bullets. Dr. Fredrickson lurched forward as his chest bloomed in red and he collapsed to the ground. The room burst out in alarm; lights and sirens blaring loudly. The door to the hallway slammed shut. Richard lumbered over to the door and tried to open it but to no avail. The officers looked around the room in confusion. Dr. Holdin looked at Dr. Fredrickson bewildered.

"What has he done?" Richards shouted at Dr. Holdin.

"I don't know. Dr. Fredrickson. Open the door immediately." Dr. Holdin demanded, shaking him by his bloodied lab coat.

Dr. Fredrickson coughed, blood pooling down the side of his face. His lips curled into a sly smile as he closed his eyes for the last time.

Charles heard the muffled sounds of an alarm from above. He pushed the specimen tube into the compartment and looked around the room. "Doctor?" he instinctively called out, knowing that Dr. Fredrickson wouldn't actually be able to hear him. He got up and went into the next room: the main control room and looked up at the staircase. Behind him the computer screen was flashing words at him in a foreign text. Despite not being fluent in it, both he and the doctor had learned enough of it to run the system. Flashing in front of him was the word 'LOCKDOWN'. He wondered what was happening above. They both knew how to activate the lockdown sequence and had practiced it numerous times. Originally a timed sequence would be implemented, but they had added an optional code function to the program so that it could be in lock down indefinitely until the code deactivated it from the outside.

He stood diligently at the screen, waiting for the clock to count down. Anytime they felt the project was at risk, they would set a timer. Dr. Fredrickson had become more skittish in his old age and many a night Charles had sent a message to his wife, telling her to not expect him for days as Dr. Fredrickson had a bad habit of mixing up the word for 'hours' and 'minutes'. His stomach grumbled, knowing he likely wasn't going to get to have her meatloaf that night.

Sighing, he went back to his work, Dr. Fredrickson still hadn't inputted a time delay so it was most likely a false alarm. Dr. Fredrickson, once calmed down, would shut off the lockdown sequence at some point. Charles was examining a specimen tube when he heard the sound of a muffled explosion followed by the room shaking slightly. He dropped the specimen tube to the ground. It shattered loudly at his feet but he paid it no notice. His heart began to race as he ran back to the control room. Again he called out to the doctor. This time his voice was laced with fear.

Charles began to run up the staircase. The

room shook with another explosion and he was almost flung from the stairwell. He gripped the railing desperately, not waiting for the shaking to stop. He was halfway up when another explosion rocked the stairwell. He screamed out at the doctor in vain. The temperature increased immensely the higher up he went, forcing him back down the stairwell. Once back at the bottom of the stairs Charles looked at the upper door as another explosion went off. He raced back into the main control room and looked at the screen knowing what to expect. Flashing on it, instead of a countdown timer, were the words, 'SYSTEM SHUTDOWN'. A single tear slid down his cheek as he knew that the doctor was dead. That he would never seen his daughter grow up and that he only had a few years at most to finish their mission.

Chapter 1

PRESENT DAY

A fresh batch of students, their first day of high school sat in the first few rows of seating in the gymnasium. Eagerly awaiting the end of announcements and the commencements of their scholarly assignment. Several rolled up the cuff of their school uniform in anticipation and stared admiringly at the barcode tattoo that had just appeared on their right wrist. Their very first 'coming of age' tattoo. The first of many that would affect the outcome of their lives. For the majority of them this was the first tattoo to have appeared on their bodies. Unless they had the unfortunate incident of having been orphaned at some point previously. Then parental unit tattoos would have appeared, dictating whom was to raise them. The parental units would then dictate their choices until they reached high school.

The kids stared in wonder at their barcodes, curious to what kind of future they would have. Knowing that the information within that very barcode would grow and change as they progressed throughout school until they finally became a contributing part of society. Little did they know that their colourful world was about to be drained into a drab existence of dull greys.

None noticed that they were the only students remaining in the gymnasium. That the higher grades had quietly left, skipping the infamous 'ceremony of selection'. The few remaining teachers had forced fake smiles plastered on their faces while the stony faced principal stood at the lectern, his gaze overlooking them sternly. To his right was a table with the school councillor seated behind it. The teachers stood held electronic clipboards in their hands, their eyes blank and empty. The principal called for the first student and a young boy, jumped from his seat, practically running up to the stage.

The boy approached the table eagerly, holding out his arm as instructed. They peeled his cuff back, revealing the barcode and placed it under the scanning device that sat next to the school councillor. It beeped loudly and the boy pulled his arm back, rolling the cuff back into place.

The silence that followed was deafening. The boy asked what happened next and the councillor immediately shushed him. From behind, one of the clipboards chirped. The teacher holding it wore faded jogging pants, a t-shirt with the school logo and a baseball cap on his head.

"Physical Education." The teacher called out and the boy looked at him confused.

The boy looked at his classmates frantically and then back at the Physical Education teacher. "But I'm going to be an architect like my father." The boy protested, his heart torn.

"Physical Education. Fall in line boy." The teacher shouted out at him. The boy, tears crawling down the sides of his face, let his arms fall slack as he took his place behind the physical education teacher. The light in his eyes snuffed out.

Student by student they were called forward, scanned and assigned into the category of their future career. Some students were bewildered by the choices made for them, while several were content at where they had been slotted. The majority of them were too simple minded to care about or know what they actually wanted. This was only the first day of many that would disappoint the few students that cared until they too, like the rest, submitted to the reality of the situation.

A couple, holding hands, walked into the Happy Caca Chinese Restaurant. The inside was as dark and dank as the night outside. A smoky haze draped thru the air while servers, donned in long dresses with high slits up the sides, buzzed about the room silently. The crowd inside appeared mildly content and not much more than that. Conversation, at best, was minimal and the atmosphere felt forced. The contentedness was masking something much darker that lingered deep within their hearts.

A petite man with a smile more fake than counterfeit money led the couple to their table. A woman appeared placing hot tea and room temperature water on the table. There were no menus. There were no specials. Only a barcode reader. They each held out their left hand, palm upwards. On the inside of their wrists were black swirl like tattoos filled with lines and dots that resembled the reaction of oil dropped in water. Once they had graduated from high school these had replaced their original barcodes. The final step into adulthood and the removal of their parental units from their lives. More wool being pulled over the proverbial eyes.

The petite man scanned their tattoos and

nodded approvingly at their 'choice' of meal and scampered off. A few moments later another server glided over and deposited plates of piping hot food on their tables. While both dishes were apparently different, they greatly resembled each other and were not visually appealing in the least. Neither knew what they had ordered, just that their bodies had chosen for them what nutrients were required at this particular moment. They dug in and ate in silence, much like everyone else in the restaurant.

At the end of the meal their plates were quickly whisked away as a coffee was deposited in front of the young man and in front of the young woman, a tea with slice of cake. As she made her way through the dessert they finally began to relax and converse. She joked about his lack of a sweet tooth and he protested, claiming to enjoy sweets more than she did. She laughed softly and playfully offered him a forkful of her cake. But before she could get the fork into his mouth a server appeared out of nowhere and swatted the fork out of her hand. The two of them sat shellshocked, as the server picked up the fork, hid it within the folds of her dress and produced a clean fork for her.

"Enjoy your cake." The server said, emphasizing the word *'your'* to the young woman before disappeared into the crowd. The young man leaned back in his chair, astounded as the young woman finished her cake in silence.

The sun shone brightly and a small breeze filled the air. The grass, now a vibrant brown, blew softly as families filled the park. Children played on the old and broken playgrounds barely holding together with what scrap materials could be found. The children squealed loudly despite many being malnourished and tiny for their age. Even with all the hardships, the children thrived the most. Their resilience gave their parents hope for a better future. Their happiness was highly infectious and that alone sustained their parents through the general misery that surrounded them, creating a veil of obliviousness.

Parents sat on benches, their conversations revolving around their children and their recent accomplishments. Both mothers and fathers adorned the benches. Whichever parent stayed home was decided shortly after childbirth and dictated by the baby tattoo on the inner right wrist. There was no sexist discrimination and often times primary parental responsibility would shift, often based on the parental units health. Places of employment would adapt to these changes seamlessly and the children would always have one parental unit with them at all times. The main importance pertaining to the needs of the child as their choices were made entirely by their parental units. When they ate, what they ate and so forth. Even what the children were to do, was mandated by barcodes on the designated primary parental unit.

The park was not only filled with parents, but an assortment of single people. This park in particular happened to be one of the more popular mating grounds within the city. When tattoos appeared on their ring finger it would indicate in which mating area they were to spend their free time. Once there they could do as they please until they found their mate. Often it only took a short walk around the park before someone would find their assigned mate. Other times it could be as long as a week. It depended on the location of their homes and place of employment in relation to the mating ground designated for them. Oftentimes people would be forced to relocate their entire lives in order to find the mate most suitable for them. Again, places of employment would seamlessly shuffle about, accommodating the change.

A young woman, 19 years of age, with vibrant red hair entered the park timidly. Her dress was too short for her height, but she couldn't afford much else. Her job barely managed to keep her fed. She had been eagerly waiting the day to find a mate, hoping she would obtain someone with a more successful vocation than hers and better financial stability. She was one of many who was not intelligent enough for post secondary education and therefore put into menial labour. She was a dishwasher at a restaurant with no hope of moving up beyond that. She looked at her right forearm hopefully as she milled about the park. Summer was a popular mating season and as such the park was filled to the brim with people.

After walking for what seemed like hours the young woman sat down on a park bench, her feet throbbing. She watched as other young women like herself walked into the park alone only to quickly leave with a man on their arms. She sighed heavily, wondering if she had misread her tattoo. Maybe she was in the wrong location.

"You too huh?" a male voice from beside her said.

She leapt out of her seat, falling off of the bench and onto the grass. The man had materialized beside her out of thin air. He was not young, like the majority of the single people wandering thru the park, but appeared to be in his late thirties. She remained on the ground, keeping her distance and looked at him skeptically.

"Aren't you a little old to be looking for a mate?" she asked him cautiously.

The man stared off into the sky and sighed softly. "My wife passed away only a week ago." He started, his eyes glistening. "I didn't expect to lose her so quickly, but her body was quite weak. We had tried many times for a child each time whenever we were supposed to, but she lost every single one. Yet she was so strong. She kept on trying. She wouldn't give up. Finally she managed to carry a baby to term. We were able to have a child, a little girl. But she died during childbirth. I lost the love of my life for another." He said choking back a sob, burying his head in his hands.

The young woman's face softened, her heart melting. She got to her feet, brushed the grass off of her clothes and sat down beside the man on the bench. "Why are you here though? Shouldn't you be with your baby?" she asked softly as she put a comforting hand on his knee.

"I will be. Soon I hope. Apparently, I need to find myself a new wife." He said holding his right hand up. On his ring finger was the same tattoo as hers, marking this particular location. He shook his head, his face grim. "I don't want to be here. I don't want a new wife. But I don't really have a choice, do I? None of us do."

She shook her head from side to side, sympathizing with him and squeezed his knee gently. She put her hand back in her own lap. "They choose because we can't."

"Can't we?" he said rhetorically. "I often wondered why we don't."

She looked at him incredulously and put a hand over his mouth. "Don't speak like that out loud. It's dangerous." She said automatically, unsure of where that came from.

He took her hand and held it gently, a smile on his face. He kissed it and set it in his lap. She blushed and squirmed uncomfortably. Part of her enjoyed this attention, but part of her also knew that unmatched mating was taboo.

"What is your profession?" he asked her.

She looked down at the ground her feet turning in slightly. "I'm a dishwasher." She said meekly.

He chuckled and squeezed her hand. "Don't be embarrassed, everyone has to do something." She mumbled something unintelligible under her breath. He leaned in closer. "What was that?" he asked.

She took a deep breath and exhaled slowly. "I wanted to be an artist." She said softly, glancing around quickly, afraid.

He leaned back and sighed. "Did you know that before you entered high school?" he asked her and she shook her head.

"I found an old book in the library of my high school. I spent a lot of time there, trying to learn and better myself after I realized that I wouldn't be going to do post secondary education. I had heard rumours of people being able to change their designated career paths if they studied hard enough." She started and turned to face him, looking him in the eyes. He was focused intently on her. "My second year of high school I found a book in the far back of the library. Buried in a box under some broken shelving, covered in years of dust. I thought that at first they were children's books because they were filled with pictures. But as I read through the books I realized that they were called, umm, whats the word. Photographs? I think that's what they called them back then. Photographs of paintings and sculptures. Things that people had created just for others to look at. They were beautiful. Some made me very happy, while others made me cry. I was so confused at how just looking at something could evoke such emotion within me. I knew then that I wanted to do the same."

"And? Did your career not change to reflect this? You studied so hard." He asked her.

She laughed sadly. "Where, today, do you see things like this?" she asked, waving a hand in front of her. "Nowhere. Only in books that are long forgotten and buried away, hidden from us all." She sighed sadly.

Impulsively he leaned over and kissed her on the lips. She pulled away from him yanking her hand from his and pressing it firmly into her lap.

"What?" he asked her softly.

"We aren't meant for each other. Look." She said as she held her hand against his. The location tattoo hadn't changed. "Only those with ring tattoos that change to match may be together." She said sadly.

"Who cares what's supposed to be. Who cares about the rules. I want to be with you." He said firmly as he drew her in for another kiss.

She resisted. "There are rules." She protested as she tried unsuccessfully to stop him from putting his lips onto hers.

"Rules are meant to be broken." He mumbled as he pressed his lips against hers again. This time she didn't hesitate.

As they were kissing a young man walked passed them. He felt his hand twitch and looked down at it as the location ring tattoo turned into a different, more intricate ring tattoo. Looking around he only saw the couple on the bench making out. Confused, he looked at his hand again and shrugged as he continued down the path away from them on the bench. So lost in the passion of their kiss the young woman never noticed the tattoo on her ring finger change to match the one on the young man as he had stood in front of them. As the young man expanded the distance between himself and the couple their matching ring tattoos faded away.

The book store was bustling as always. End of summer symbolized the beginning of the new studies and as the only book store in the city it was always quite busy. Books were so incredibly scarce that people were only able to buy what they needed. Educational units provided only the most basic of books required in the streamlined classes and the libraries consisted only of what few books had survived over the years. Reading was a frivolous hobby for only the rich and government workers. The proprietor of the bookstore stood on the second floor, watching over as students milled about in his store. Like little robots they beelined for the books they required, went back to the counter, got scanned and left the store quickly. In and out. Efficiently, quickly and quietly. Just the way he liked it.

The band symbolizing his status as a

proprietor on his forearm buzzed briefly and he glanced down at the checkout counter below him. One of the lines had come to a complete stop as the patron at the counter was awkwardly trying to make a purchase they were unable to complete. Most likely they were short of funds. It happened occasionally where a child was put into a career path above the means of their current parental units. He smiled as he made his way down to the checkout counter. He would need to gather the career details of the child and create a future account for the child. Knowing that once the child had entered his or hers designated career they would be able to pay off the purchases then. This wouldn't be the first book the child would likely need and not be able to pay for now. He would track the purchase, deem the child's account acceptable regardless of their parental units funds and the government would reimburse him for the time being.

When he got to the checkout counter he smiled at the young boy and assured him that they would be able to process his purchase. That this happened often and wouldn't be a problem. He scanned the book and the image of the boys parental units barcode. He looked at the scanner, confused by what it was displaying. Again, he scanned the book and the young boys parental units barcode. The boy began to squirm uncomfortably, the crowd behind him beginning to murmur to themselves and sneak glances at him.

"Can I get the book please?" the boy asked, gripping it tightly in his hands. The owner kept a grip on the book as well.

"Well son, it seems that we have ourselves a small predicament." The owner started, his voice growing stern.

"There shouldn't be a problem. My parents have the funds to buy this book." The boy said quietly.

"Is this book meant for yourself? Or perhaps someone else?" the owner asked a smile plastered on his face. He leaned over to the clerk beside him and whispered something into his ear. The clerk ran off quickly.

The boy looked from the book to the exit of the store. His grip loosened on the book but the proprietor grabbed him by the wrist. The boy yelped loudly.

"I don't want it anymore. Please let me go." The boy cried out.

The owner shook his head from side to side. "We all have rules to follow. Regardless of who your parental units may be."

The boy yanked his arm free and went crashing down into the crowd that had gathered behind him. Pushing on the bodies beneath him he quickly got to his feet and ran for the exit. Just as he had thought himself in the clear two government military officers burst thru the door and roughly grabbed him by the arms. They looked at the proprietor who nodded and they just as quickly as they had entered they left with the boy kicking and screaming the whole time.

As the boy's cries died off the entire store was silent with shock. The owner clapped his hands together loudly and smiled. "Ladies and gentlemen. I do apologize for that small intrusion. That child was attempting to break the rules and purchase a book beyond his capabilities. Since our resources are limited we must always adhere to the rules of only purchasing what is required for you. Don't worry, he will be taken to his parental units and scolded appropriately. Lets continue on with our day and our purchases." He said with a smile before turning his attention to the next patron in line. "M'am, what can I help you with today?"

The silence broken, the crowd slowly lumbered back into their respective lines and resumed their purchasing. As they left the store, the incident became a far off and distant memory that quickly evaporated from their minds.

* * *

A young couple lay in their bed, naked except for the sheets strewn haphazardly about their bodies. The woman rolled onto her side and curled into the man's body. They were both sweaty, their skins flush with a post coitus glow. He wrapped his arm around her waist and pulled her closer, squeezing her gently.

"Do you think it worked?" she asked him.

He shrugged his shoulders. "It should. We went about it as soon as we saw the baby tattoo."

She rolled over to face him. "Its a good thing it shows up on both of us. I would have hated to have to call your boss and tell him why you had to leave work early."

They both laughed. "Do you think we should do it again for good measure? Just in case it didn't work?" he asked almost too eagerly, pushing his body up against hers. She could feel that he was ready to go again.

"Hmmm, lets see." She said teasingly holding her arm out to see the tattoo on her forearm. He held his arm beside hers. They had matching symbols of the old gemini astrology symbol. Twins intertwined with each other. One male, one female. His tattoo faded away completely as the male twin on her arm faded away leaving only the female. She squealed. "A baby girl.

What I've always wanted."

He growled softly rolling her onto her back and crawling on top of her. Her eyes grew wide as she smiled from ear to ear. "Lets see if we can give her a brother right away." He said with a grin.

Chapter 2

The bar, like every other establishment in town, was poorly lit, dank and dirty. You could barely navigate yourself through it from one end to the other without tripping on something hidden in the shadows. The windows were papered over with old newspapers preventing any outside light from trickling in. The floors were sticky despite having just been cleaned earlier in the day. What little decor was left on the walls hung lifelessly clinging to a time long since gone. The bartender was the cleanest thing in the room and his hair was filled with dirt and lice, His clothes hadn't been laundered in several days and the stink that wafted from him helped to cover the decaying smell of old, homemade alcohol. Bars were, by far and large, in all cities run illegally. The consumption of alcohol however, was not. Mainstream alcohol was made, distributed and regulated by the government. It was a rarity in the average household. Used primarily as a formality amongst larger businesses. As such, establishments that illegally served alcohol flew under the radar of the government and lacked the proper 'Health and Safety' standards. Standards that were so low their existence was a running joke.

Regardless, the bar was packed. The crew in the back could barely make the alcohol supply fast enough to keep up with the demand. It was not only a place to drown the sorrows of your meaningless life, but a popular distribution place for illicit drugs, paraphernalia and work. The only two rules were you had to buy alcohol in order to stay inside and puking was to be contained to the supplied troughs. You could nurse a single drink all night if you so desired so long as you never had an empty glass.

Like a typical weekday, there were several regular clients utilizing the bar for a quick drink before heading home. From the usual business men who had developed a taste for the drink to those too depressed to function unless they were in an alcoholic induced stupor. In the mens washroom you could find any drug that you could imagine while in the women's washroom you would find books, cigarettes and other items not commonly available amongst the public. Physical currency had died out decades ago and all transactions were tracked via your barcodes. So the currency for such goods was strictly on a bartering basis of physical goods. You could never know if the items you were bartering with would be worth a lot or a little. Sometimes men would come in hoping for a quick hit but leave with enough supply to last them a month. It varied entirely on supply and demand as well as the whim and fancies of the those dealing.

In the far back reaches of the bar was a non electronic message board divided into multiple slots. It was sorted in accordance to job detail and difficulty. Here, people who refused to conform to their designated career path could find menial labour to help pay the bills. Most of the jobs paid legitimate currency. The scanners these wealthy employers used could scramble the signals so it would appear that you were working in your 'designated area' regardless of what you had done for them. The pay was usually significantly less due to the risk to the employer, but work was abundant enough that you could scrape together a meagre living. The higher paying the job the more illegal it was. These jobs were often attended to by a very few select individuals. These jobs were marked off in black envelopes on the lowest rung of slots. You never opened a black envelope unless you were willing to cross that line. Not even to sneak a glance at what the job could be. It was a code of honour that no one broke.

A man with short brown hair, a full reddish brown beard and a scar that ran down his one cheek walked into the bar. Both his beard and scar hid the youthful glint in his eyes. He wore new, barely broken in jeans, red sneakers and a long forgotten band shirt under his brown hoodie. Hidden beneath this casual attire was an arsenal of weapons that would make a normal person wet themselves. He went to the bar and slapped a deck of cards onto the counter. The bartender opened it, peered inside and nodded. He disappeared into the back for a moment then reappeared with a pint glass filled to the brim with a murky looking beer. He handed it the man who then proceeded to the back of the room to the message board.

As the man got closer the group of people huddling around it took notice and quickly dispersed. The man scanned the board as he drank his beer and finally settled on one of the elusive black envelopes. He opened it, read it, nodded with approval and slide it into an inner pocket. He took another drink of his beer and selected another black enveloped. He too, put that one in his jacket pocket and then a third envelope.

A man, also holding a pint of murky beer, slapped him on his shoulder. "C'mon Denis, leave something for the rest of us."

Denis turned to face his childhood friend, Jeffery, a physically small, scrawny and childlike built man but with the brains of a hundred men. His glasses were thicker than they needed to be and gave him bug like eyes. His clothes were in desperate need of being cleaned, as did he.

"Jeffery, mate, have you not heard of this thing called a bath. Been around since the dawn of time." Denis said, waving his hand in front of his face. "You stink."

Jeffery shrugged his shoulders and ran a hand through his long dirty hair. Denis grabbed a few limp strands and let them fall down in a clump from his fingers. "I think you may be growing life in here. You know thats not how procreation works right?"

Jeffery slapped Denis's shoulder and went to snatch the envelope from Denis's hand but Denis pulled his hand back quickly and slapped Jeffery on either cheek with it instead. He slid the envelope into his jacket and produced a different envelope.

"This one is more up your alley." Denis said as Jeffery eagerly plucked the envelope out of his hands.

Jeffery opened it up, scanned the contents inside and nodded with approval. He looked up at Denis fondly. "You could easily do this one too, you know. It pays a lot."

"Yeah, but it would take me a lot longer than you to translate. They don't say how big the manuscript is. Last one you did was well over a hundred pages. For you that's a weeks worth, for me at least a month. Money isn't as big if it takes your whole damn life to do the job. Besides, you know I prefer the easy gigs." He said with a sly smile.

"You mean you like killing people better." Jeffery said with a scoff.

"Only smart asses like you." Denis replied as he squeezed Jeffery's shoulders. "C'mon, let me buy you a drink." He said as he pulled Jeffery away from the message board, now void of black envelopes.

They sat down at a table near the board and Denis waved a hand in the air. When the server looked over at him he stuck 2 fingers in the air and she disappeared with a nod into the crowd. Moments later two more murky beers as well as a bowl of something that resembled pretzels appeared on the table. They took their beers and toasted each other before they drank. Denis set his pint down and sighed happily. Jeffery scanned the crowd.

"The crowd keeps getting bigger yet the jobs keep getting less and less." Jeffery mumbled.

"Tell me about it. This keeps up I'll have to start keeping the luxuries down." Denis said rolling his eyes dramatically. Jeffery burst out with laughter. Denis gave him a knowing grin before he laughed as well. Luxuries for him meant nothing more than prostitutes and drugs. He had everything he needed for the time being and whenever he needed something more he simply took it. He slept on a pullout couch in their apartment and was quite content with that. Jeffery, on the other hand, had a large collection of rare books. He had come from a wealthy family and before he defected he had squirrelled away an immense number of his books into a hideout that only the two of them knew about.

It was from this collection that they had both learned countless languages lost to the present time and had educated themselves in a variety of technology and skills long forgotten to the world. Jeffery had a keen intellect for studying and for every language that Denis mastered, Jeffery mastered ten. Jeffery also had a keen eye for detail and was incredibly meticulous. From this Jeffery had started translating documents for the government on the side and many other businesses eager to uncover past mysteries. He also created false documents for the various factions to leave 'undiscovered', hoping that the enemy would find them and be led astray. Jeffery laughed every time he was hired to translate documents that he had previously falsified.

Denis had a mind for building and tinkering. He had developed a list of clientele eager for his electronic and robotic creations. Although mostly harmless, they were ultimately illegal and as time went on, the request for such 'toys' became scarce. In his free time he had studied and trained a variety of martial arts and had a diverse range of skills, strength and weaponry knowledge. Even with the lack of identical weapons today to reference the two of them had fashioned ones similar enough that he was able to utilize. Despite selling some of these said weapons, Denis still had the edge over the majority of the illicit since he was the only one who knew how to properly utilize the weapons to their fullest capabilities.

A sudden hush went over the bar as the doors burst open and two men adorned in full length black trench coats, sunglasses, and fedora type hats sauntered in. The bartender greeted the gentlemen and offered them a drink on the house. They shook their heads and scanned the crowd. They made a beeline straight for Denis and Jeffery. Jeffery squirmed in his seat until Denis kicked him in the shins. Denis tipped his mug towards the men and greeted them as they stood in front of their table. The crowd around them quickly dispersed like cockroaches in a brightly lit room. Denis peered around the room and joked that the men could clear a room faster than the plague.

Looking unimpressed the man took the pint glass from Denis's hand and sniffed it, his nose crinkling. He drank the remainder of the beer and slammed the glass onto the table. "Still drinking this swill, eh Private?" he said smugly. Jeffery's eyes darted nervously but Denis had plastered a fake smile onto his face.

"Only the best for me and my mate." Denis said quietly. "What can I do for you today, Lieutenant Colonel? Can we do it quickly? You're scaring the locals and its bad for business."

The Lieutenant Colonel reached inside Denis's jacket and pulled out the two black envelopes that were stashed inside. He opened the envelopes and read them to himself. As he scanned them he nodded with mocking approval.

"This one pays the most and you only have to kill his wife. Not too bad for a days work. This would be what, his third wife to have 'died of mysterious circumstances'?" he said smugly. "You've already killed the first two, correct?"

Denis shrugged his shoulders, leaned back into his chair and waved a hand in the air. The server quickly deposited four mugs of beer on the table and scurried off. Denis took one up, shoved another into Jeffery's shaking hands and offered the other two towards the Lieutenant Colonel. The Lieutenant Colonel crumpled the envelopes and let them fall to the floor.

"We will catch you in the act one of these days." The Lieutenant Colonel said, his voice trembling with anger.

"If you say so." Denis said smugly, a sly smile on his lips as he drank his beer. He downed it in one go and then took one of the untouched beers. "You don't mind, do you? Don't want good beer to go to waste."

The Lieutenant Colonel slammed his fist on the table. "Don't you mock me. Mark my words. I will be the one to take you down."

"Your threats are getting to be quite a bore. So, tell me Conrad, why are you really here? It can't be just for small talk." Denis said, continuing to drink his beer. "Am I under arrest for something I didn't do again?"

The Lieutenant Colonel, Conrad, grabbed Denis by the throat and squeezed it. Denis choked, the beer spilling from his mouth.

Conrad pulled him out of the chair and slammed Denis up against the wall. Denis mumbled incoherently, trying to get Conrad's attention.

Conrad leaned in. "I'm sorry, did you say something? Its quite difficult to hear you. Speak up." He said, his voice dripping with sarcasm.

Denis tried to speak, but his face was red and his words mere sputters of inaudible sound. Conrad sighed and loosened his grip slightly. "Try again Private dumbass." He said.

Denis looked Conrad squarely in the eyes, his hand still holding his pint of beer as he simply said. "Jeffery. Beer."

Jeffery leapt to his feet and took the pint glass out of Denis's hand. His hand now free Denis punched Conrad in the gut and caught him as Conrad slumped over. His hand let go of Denis's throat and his partner immediately drew out his gun and aimed it at Denis's head. Denis, still rubbing his throat gingerly, cleared his throat and nodded his head slightly. The soldier looked around to see the entire bar turning to face him, each and every single person armed with some type of weapon in their hands.

The bartender called out from behind the bar. "We don't want to be a hinderance to your procedures officer. But last I checked, police brutality is still illegal. You may leave this establishment peacefully, but you will do so alone."

The soldiers looked around bewildered. Conrad put a hand on the soldiers arm, lowering the gun. Conrad hissed at the solider to leave. The soldier put his gun away and propped Conrad up on his arm. The crowd parted slightly to allow for them to leave. Once they had departed Denis reached inside his pocket and pulled out another deck of cards. He tossed it to the bartender and shouted out that the next round was on him. The crowd cheered as the bartender nodded, a sly smile on dancing across his eyes. Denis leaned down, picked up the crumpled envelopes and flattened them out. He put them back into his hoodie. Jeffery handed him back his beer and stared at him incredulously.

"You're still going to do them?" he asked and Denis nodded. "But he'll know that it's you."

"Knowing and proving are two very different things, my friend. And it'll kill Conrad not being able to prove it was me." Denis said, a mischievous grin on his face. "Besides, someone has to earn money for food. You keep wasting it on books." He said mockingly as Jeffery glared at him. "Seriously, you look like a rabid chipmunk with those things." The server looked at him confused as she set down more beer and asked what a chipmunk was. They looked at each other and laughed. She shook her head and left them to their own musings.

"Do you ever wonder what it is that they are feeding us?" Jefferey asked suddenly. "Given that animals don't exist anymore except in the inhabitable lands."

Denis chuckled. "No and I am grateful that no one has written about that shit. God knows you would have the book on it, have read the shit out of it and then neither of us would be able to ever eat again." He shuddered.

Jeffery laughed. "So very, very true." He lifted his beer and proposed a toast. "To your bravery that dances at the fine line of insanity." They toasted and drank, late into the night.

The sounds of someone scuffling about the room brought Denis out of his slumber. He immediately grabbed a knife and waved it haphazardly in front of him.

"Really? After all the work I did to get him to perform, this is the thanks I get?" the blonde prostitute said, rolling her eyes as she gathered her clothing.

Denis smacked his lips and rubbed his eyes, almost poking himself with the knife. With one eye squinting he looked at her through the darkness of early morning. "Suzette?" he asked groggily.

She leaned over and kissed him on the lips. "Mmm hmm. Gotta get back to the husband before he wakes up. Thanks for the night luv." She called out a farewell to Jeffery as she left the living room.

As she left Jeffery walked into the living room, a towel wrapped around his waist and water glistening off of his skin. Denis looked up at him approvingly. "You showered?" he asked incredulously.

"Twice." Jeffery said proudly.

Denis looked at him, his eyes twinkling with astonishment. A young girl's voice could be heard calling out for Jeffery. Denis's eyes popped wide opened. He pointed to Jeffery, then to his lower extremities and then back to his upper half, then out the doorway towards the mysterious voice. He gave Jeffery a look of disbelief and Jeffery whipped his towel off and threw it in Denis's face.

Denis gagged, pulled the towel off and threw it back at him. "Dude cover that thing up. Its disgusting."

"That's not what she said." Jeffery laughed as Denis groaned, collapsing back onto his bed. Jeffery sauntered off, wiggling his lower extremities for effect, making Denis gag even more.   Jeffery suddenly stopped and turned back to face Denis. He rushed back towards the couch.

"Seriously, I don't want to see that. Ever. Especially first thing in the morning." Denis said groaning.

Jeffery knelt down in front of him and stared at Denis. "Its afternoon." He stated matter of fact, pushing his glasses up further on the bridge of his nose.

"I don't care. Its touching me. Get it off." Denis said gagging.

"Shut up and don't move." Jefferey ordered and Denis immediately froze. It wasn't like Jeffery to order him around like that. The girl called out to Jeffery again and he barked at her to shut her yap and wait. She squeaked out a reply but clammed up. Jeffery grabbed Denis's face and turned it to the side. He grabbed his towel from the floor and rubbed it on Denis's cheek. Denis grimaced and Jeffery told him to stop being a baby. Finally Jeffery sat down on the bed beside Denis and simply stared at him with wonder and shock.

Denis put a pillow on Jeffery's junk. "What the hell is wrong with you?" Denis asked, rubbing his cheek gingerly.

"You might want to look in the mirror." Jeffery managed to say softly.

Denis got up and went to the bathroom. He growled loudly. "What the fuck is this bullshit. Did you draw on me dumbass? This isn't funny." Denis called out to him.

"I didn't do it. And its not coming off." Jeffery said, now standing behind Denis in the bathroom, the towel finally wrapped around his waist again.

"Did we go get tattoos? No. Why would we do something like that? I mean I know why we'd do that, but my face? No one gets tattoos on their face." Denis muttered, mostly to himself.

"It couldn't have been done last night. Doesn't look fresh, its fully healed.

Besides, no one is dumb enough to ink someone on the face. There isn't enough money in the whole world to convince someone to mark you like that." Jeffery said, his voice filling with concern.

"How the hell am I going to work like this?"

"You could cover your face? I mean, you usually do don't you?" Jefferey asked, poking at the tattoo on his cheek. Denis swatted Jeffery's hand away and tried to rub the tattoo off unsuccessfully.

Denis shot him a dirty look. "Sunglasses are usually enough to hide your identity, Conrad and his buddies aren't that smart." A light bulb suddenly went off and Denis's eyes sparked with life. "Conrad. He must have done this somehow. He wanted to mark me."

"Denis. That's impossible."

"Is it? I'm sure that a crooked officer with enough money could get anyone in the black market to tattoo my face." He picked at the tattoo and trying to peel it off like a scab.

"There's no one in this city that would risk crossing paths with you. You know that. You are too well respected and feared." Jeffery said.

Denis put his hands on either side of the sink as he slumped his head over. Jeffery put a hand on his shoulder and Denis angrily shoved him into the wall. Jeffery cowered as Denis swore and punched the wall beside the mirror. The young girl in Jeffery's room squeaked. "Dammit, I'm sorry Jeffery. Its just…" he said, his voice trailing off.

Jeffery took a hesitant step towards Denis. "I understand. I really do. Just lay low for now and I'll figure something out." He said and Denis looked at him curiously. "Something about this seems familiar. There's something niggling at the back of my mind. I must have read about it somewhere at some point." Again, he put a hand on Denis shoulder. "We'll figure it out and fix it. I promise." He said as Denis punched the mirror with his fist, the glass shattering and falling into the sink.

Chapter 3

Denis sat on the couch surrounded by piles upon piles of books. He was currently trudging his way thru a copy of 'Ripley's Believe it or Not". He slammed the book shut and threw it across the floor cursing loudly. Jeffery shouted out to him to not damage the books. Denis told him to go fuck himself as Jeffery walked into the room, book in hand. He went to the discarded book, finding its spine now bent. He scolded Denis as he picked up the book and put it on the pile of already read books. Denis got up in a huff and grabbed his hoodie.

"Where are you going?" Jeffery asked.

"Out."

"Where exactly?"

"Christ, what are you? My mom?" Denis huffed, zipping his hoodie up to his neck as he pulled his hoodie over his head.

"Here, there, anywhere, I can't stay inside anymore. I'm going stir crazy." Denis said as he slipped into his shoes. Jeffery stood in front of him, blocking his way. "Don't even try to stop me." He said angrily.

"I'm not going to. Just wait a minute. Let me fix you up." Jeffery said, disappearing briefly before returning with a bag of assorted small jars. He began to apply makeup directly onto the tattoo.

Denis pushed Jeffery away, grabbing the hand that held a sponge. "What the hell is this shit?" he demanded, rubbing his cheek.

Jeffery slapped Denis's hand away and resumed applying the makeup. "It's called makeup. I read about it. Girls used to put it on before going outside, to hide imperfections." He said sternly.

Denis scoffed. "I know a lot of girls that could use that."

Jeffery gave him a wry look. "Maybe we should quit our lives of crime and mass produce makeup. What do you think? Perhaps we could make a killing before the government took it away from us?" He took a step back and admired his handiwork with a smile.

Denis wrinkled his nose. "It feels weird."

Jeffery slapped his hand again. "Don't touch it. It'll come off."

"What's the point in that? Wouldn't girls want it to stay on?" Denis said scrunching his cheek.

"If it was permanent then women would only need to buy a little of it. Then we'd be out of business before we even started. We want to make money don't we?" Jeffery said mockingly and paused, scrutinizing his work. "Thats as good as its going to get. Thankfully your beard sort of hides it. Its late enough out that people aren't as likely to notice. Just don't let anyone get a close look of your face. The one side is a bit lighter than the other. I was a little off in matching your skin tone."

Denis looked at him incredulously. "You made it?"

Jeffery nodded. "Don't know how long it'll take for me to figure out a permanent solution. Figured the sooner I get you out of the house, the sooner I can focus on finding a real solution."

Denis abruptly hugged him and Jeffery stood awkwardly, his arms trapped at his sides. When Denis broke off the hug Jeffery patted him on the shoulder and handed Denis his tools of the trade. "Now be a good boy and go kill someone. Get rid of that pent up energy. You're driving me bat shit crazy."

Denis assembled the weapons throughout his

attire, a healthier glow already on his face. He smiled as he pulled out the still crumpled envelopes. As he left the room Jeffery called out to him. "Don't forget to bring home supper. I want Chinese."

Denis stood in a room watching a woman lying in her bed, her husband standing beside him. The life slowly seeping out of her eyes. As she finally took her last breath her eyes slowly closed. Denis waited a moment, then with gloved hands he checked her wrist for a pulse. Satisfied he looked at his employer, her husband, and nodded. He then went about the room, dressing it up. He opened a bottle champagne and poured a small amount into a glass. He then pulled a flask out of his jacket and poured the champagne from the glass into the flask. He took a swig of it, nodded his head with approval and filled his flask with champagne. He took the glass to the now dead woman and pressed her lips onto the rim, leaving a smear of lip print on it. He fashioned her hand into a makeshift grip and held it over the stem of the glass firmly for a few moments. Then he loosen his grip on her hand and set the glass and her hand on the bed to lay naturally in death. Her fingers uncurled slightly.

He produced a small baggie of pills out of an

inner jacket pocket and left it opened on the nightstand beside the bed next to the opened bottle of champagne. He crushed two pills and sprinkled some of it on the floor next to the bed and trickled a small amount into the champagne glass she still held. On the desk, across from the bed, he found the note that he had forced her to write covered in her now dried tears. He turned it slightly askew and set the pen on it. He scanned the room for any signs of distress and was satisfied that he found none. He did find a diary that he pocketed. He didn't know what was written in it, but did not want to take the chance that anything contradictory was written within it.

He turned to face his employer. "Wait an hour before contacting the authorities. In fact, I would recommend that you go to a bar or some other establishment outside of this room until at least that much time has passed. Then return, find her and contact the authorities. If you contact them too soon, they may be able to revive her."

"I know the drill." The husband said with a smirk as he held out a small handheld scanner. Denis pulled his sleeve up to reveal his barcode. The man scanned it and thus depositing his pay. "Whats up with your face, are you alright?"

Denis pulled his ball cap further down,

mumbled something unintelligible and rushed off. He hurried down the stairs out of the hotel and took off for the nearest alley. Finding a broken window he removed his ball cap and took a closer look at his cheek. The room had been quite warm and he had sweated a fair bit. As a result, some of the make up had melted off in streaks. He tried to smooth it out but only resulted in making it look worse. He sighed, knowing that Jeffery would be pissed if he didn't at least bring home dinner, but he didn't know how he could with the tattoo starting to show. He felt thru his pockets until he found a knife with a taped up handle. He removed a small bit of the tape and stuck it directly over the tattoo. He looked into the glass again and although he looked incredibly odd and was certain to draw attention to himself, he rather it be for looking like a weirdo then risk someone seeing the tattoo.

"Honey, I'm home." Denis shouted out as he waltzed through the front door. He immediately tripped over a stack of books piled high and went flying ass over tea kettle. "Hay amina koyayim." he swore. He managed to save the bag of food but took out the books instead. "What the hell are you doing Jeffery? I thought we weren't redecorating until spring." He shouted out cheerfully.

Jeffery, his nose buried in a book, came around the corner. He looked up briefly. "Why are you so cheerful all of a sudden?" he asked. Denis waved the bag of food in front of his face and Jeffery inhaled deeply. "Is that—?" he petered off as he began to drool. Denis nodded. "How? We can't afford that. Who the hell did you kill?"

Denis roared with laughter and pointed to his face. On it was his make shift bandage of tape overtop the melting makeup. Jeffery looked at him curiously. "What is that?"

"That," Denis started pulling out one of his knives, "was part of my knife. This stuff started melting off so I put this" he said waving the knife about, "on my face. The servers at the restaurant thought I was injured. So I got the royal treatment." He finished with a smile as he the set the bag down on the coffee table atop of some books.

Jeffery grumbled as he picked the bag up, removed the books and set the bag back down. Denis plopped down onto the couch and put his feet, still wearing shoes, onto a stack of books. Jeffery kicked his legs off and removed the books, grumbling. Denis laughed. He leaned over, opened the bag and pulled out a spread fit for a king. The two of them had scarcely eaten over the last few days and had not eaten this well since Jeffery had last lived at home with his parental units. That was several years ago. The aroma emanating from the food made theirs mouths salivate. There was even plastic utensils in the bag instead of the usual wooden sticks. A leftover treat from the past.

They dug in hungrily, eating like starving animals on their way to the heavens, noisily slurping their food. When they had both eaten their fill, Denis abruptly jumped up. He reached into his hoodie and pulled out a bottle of champagne. Identical to the one he had left behind in the hotel room. He popped the cork and took a big drink from the bottle before passing it over to Jeffery. Jeffery hesitantly sniffed it before trying a small sip. Another leftover and expensive relic from the past.

Once they had finished eating Jeffery grabbed the book he had been reading and resumed his research. Denis leaned back and rubbed his cheek with a piece of paper. He looked at the makeup that came off and chuffed. "Girls really wore this shit?" he asked Jeffery.

"Uh huh." Jeffery answered absently.

"Everyday?"

"Yup."

"Why?" Denis asked.

"Mating."

Denis sat up straight and looked at Jeffery with surprise. "This? They used this to mate?" he asked incredulously.

Jeffery chuckled. "If what I read was correct, the prettier you were the better a man you got. Better meaning richer. They didn't mate like we do. It was difficult. You had to search far and wide for a mate. Just to find the best one possible."

Denis shook his head. "That be some crazy shit."

Jeffery nodded in agreement, his nose still buried in the book. "I concur. I think —" he suddenly stopped talking, his jaw dropping. Denis laughed and lifted Jeffery's chin, closing his mouth.

"Aww, did Jeffy poo find a picture too naughty for his widdle brain to comprehend?" Denis said mockingly as he took the book out of his hands. He looked at it, unable to decipher the words. "What is this gibberish?"

Jeffery regained his composure and snatched the book back. "This gibberish, might be the answer."

"You can read gibberish?" Denis said laughing as he drank more champagne directly from the bottle.

"Denis. This gibberish talks about tattoos that mysteriously appear."

Denis slowly set the bottle of champagne down on the table. He felt his heart lurch. "Don't mess with me Jeffery."

"I'm not. I'm serious. Look." He said pushing the book into Denis's face.

"I don't read gibberish. What does it say?" Denis asked, moving in closer to Jeffery who placed the book on their laps in front of them.

"You used to be able to read gibberish." Jeffery said haughtily.

Denis glared at him. "Just read it."

"The entry—" he started.

"Entry?" Denis said interrupting him.

"Its a journal, a scientific journal, from what I have read of it so far."

"Holy shit." Denis said with disbelief. "What are the chances?"

"Not so good given that the most physical and tangible books have been destroyed with time, yet also fairly good given my extensive collection." Jeffery said smugly. When they first took possession of the building they had only been able to acquire a single room. Over time they had taken over half of the building, six floors in total. Most of them were dedicated to Jeffery's book collection. Yet they had chosen to live in the same apartment. Denis had always told Jeffery that he couldn't leave him alone. Truth was Denis looked after Jeffery. It not for him Jeffery wouldn't remember to shower let alone feed himself.

"So what does it say about my tattoo." Denis asked.

"It doesn't talk about your tattoo specifically, at least not yet. Its currently talking about all of our tattoos. Apparently a doctor, this great research scientist, released a toxin in the air that created the tattoos." Jeffery said as he read the entry.

"We both know that. Everyone knows that. The tattoos were given to us to make life easier. To prevent us from making the wrong choices and allowing us to live complete and fulfilled lives. To help keep humanity as a whole, ridding us of our selfish impulses." Denis said mockingly, regurgitating the lessons that had been instilled since birth.

"Right. It says that at first, only adults were affected by the toxin. It was later discovered that upon puberty adolescents were physically capable of manifesting the tattoos. Prior to that their bodies weren't healthy or strong enough to undergo that transformation." Jeffery read. He skimmed through the next paragraph and flipped the page. "There was apparently several rounds of the toxin before they had mastered the full capabilities of programming the code. Christ, they hadn't even tested it before they used it on us. We could have all been killed."

"Don't think that would have been such a bad thing considering." Denis said shrugging his shoulders.

"Don't talk like that Denis. Death is never the answer."

"Tell me more." Denis said.

Jeffery read through the entries, skimming them, flipping page after page. "They streamlined the main tattoo to be barcodes. Allowed for more control by the government. Originally symbols that were easily identifiable appeared. He says that when you went to eat the tattoo of your meal would appear. The government didn't like this, they wanted more control over the citizens, to better prevent the current devastation from getting worse. So they turned the main tattoo into a barcode. Relationship and procreation related circumstances remained as appearing tattoos since it was too expensive and troublesome for everyone to own a scanner." He flipped to the next page. "Hmmm interesting. Apparently the first round of toxins simply motivated you to work. Humanity had become completely dependent on those robots that you like to build."

Denis rolled his eyes. "If I could build a robot to do everything, why wouldn't I want to depend on it?"

Jeffery flipped through the journal until he got to the end. Denis looked at him expectantly and Jeffery just shrugged his shoulders. Denis took the journal from him and flipped thru the pages. "There has to be more to it than this."

"I can look to see if I have another of his journals." Jeffery said, getting to his feet.

"Wait. What's this?" Denis asked pointing to an entry in the journal.

"He's just talking about how they're modifying the toxins for another round." Jeffery said. "Nothing more."

"No, not that. This." He said pointing to a series of symbols at the bottom of the page. "They look like numbers don't they?" He flipped forward to another entry and pointed to more similar symbols. "They're scattered throughout the journal."

Jeffery snatched the journal from his hands. "They're probably just a date marker..." he said trailing off again. "Damn, I'm an idiot." He muttered to himself.

"What? What is it?" Denis asked frantically.

"He's dated each entry at the bottom, not the top. But not every entry is dated. Only specific entries. Each time he talks about modifying the toxins." He dropped the journal onto the floor and dashed out of the room.

"Jeffery?" Denis called out after him, picking up the journal. He followed him into the next room and down a staircase to the floor below. "Jeffery?"

"I think I've seen those numerals before. A long time ago. In a fairy tale book." Jeffery called out from below. The floor below them was entirely dedicated to Jeffery's books. Denis crouched down over an opening in the floor.

"What am I, a fairy now?" he called out laughing. "You're not going to find any answers in a fairy tale book."

Jeffery emerged from the staircase behind Denis with several books in hand. Jeffery took the journal from Denis and sat down on the floor beside him.

Denis indicated their apartment. "We have a couch."

"Find the first set of numerals." Jeffery ordered and Denis complied. Taking the journal back and flipping thru the pages until found the first entry. "Show them to me." Denis held the page out to him and Jeffery flipped through the fairy tale book until he found the right page. The fairy tale book was numbered using numerals identical to that in the journals entries. Jeffery scanned the page smiling.

"Holy shit. I am a fairy." Denis said stunned.

Jeffery laughed. "I think you're safe from that

fate. Look." He said as he pulled on a tab, causing a small boy to jump over a candlestick.

"What is that supposed to mean? I'm going to burn my dick?" Denis said skeptically.

"I don't think its meant to help you. Its meant to help hide."

"Hide what?"

"Clues." Jeffery said with a smile as he ripped the boy out of the book. Denis jumped at the noise and Jeffery laughed. He saw nothing in the mechanism that moved the boy, but when he pried the paper apart he found a folded up piece of paper underneath. He unfolded it and found it written in the same scripture as the journal. Excited, Denis took the book and began to flip thru the pages, looking for more pop ups. Jeffery slammed the book shut on his hands. Denis yelped aloud and rubbed his fingers tenderly.

"What was that for?"

"Look in the journal. Find the next entry with numerals." Jeffery ordered.

Denis found the next one. The numerals matched that of the first entry. He shrugged his shoulders.

Jeffery shook his head. Without removing the pop up he pried the side open to reveal another folded up piece of paper. Denis looked surprised.

"If he went to the trouble of writing this in code, he wouldn't want it falling into the wrong hands, would he? Nor would it be that easy to put together. Look at the numerals again."

Denis looked at the first entry's numerals and then at the second entry's. Both had the three digit numeral coding, but they were also followed by a series of letters. They looked at the first clue and read the title of the story. The letters "JCK" from the title matched the letters in the first clue. The second clue they found "BNM".

"We got lucky with the first clue. They probably need to be in a specific order, otherwise they own't make sense when put together. If we find them out of order we may never understand what he's written." Jeffery's nose crinkled briefly. "Although I'm not sure why certain letters are missing. I think the ones he's left out belong to a specific group in that language."

"How many fairy tale books do you have?" Denis asked.

"Hundreds. At the very least. But only six that have those pop up thingies." Jeffery said.

Denis sighed. The journal although sparse in text was quite thick and every other entry pretty much had a numerical sequence written with it.

"You start finding the clues, in the proper

order, and I'll start translating what you find."
Jeffery said and Denis sighed as he began to flip
through the fairy tale books.

Jeffery disappeared briefly, only to return
with a pot, a handful of papers and some
matches.

"What are you doing with that?" Denis asked.
Jeffery put the paper in the pot and lit them with
the match. They watched the fire quickly burn
until nothing was left other than the ashes.
Jeffery spit into the pot and using a stick mixed
his saliva with the ashes. He then took the first
clue they found and marked it with a symbol at
the top right hand corner. Denis looked at him
with question.

"We need a way to keep them in order, do we
not? You remember this language, yes?" Jeffery
asked and Denis nodded. "Now find more
clues."

Denis continued to read thru the fairy tale
books, pulling out clue after clue. Jeffery would
label them accordingly as he continued
translating the clues. Denis quickly discovered
that the scientist hid clues in multiple books
with the same page number and that they were
missing about two other fairy tale books.
Whenever they noticed they were missing pages
they would indicate so on the preceding pages.

A few hours into their search Denis stood up

and stretched his legs. "Tell me you found something useful."

Jeffery also stood up, scrunching his face. "I think I have. But it may also be a ruse."

"What's a ruse?" Denis demanded. "Look at my face and tell me this is a ruse."

"He's incredibly vague in these entires. He keeps talking about saving humanity and the government trying to take over the world and some secret project. Its mostly ranting and ravings of what seems like a mad scientist." Jeffery said.

"Oh, so we're reading your journal now, are we?" Denis said, a giant grin growing on his face.

Jeffery ignored him. "The only thing of interest that I can find regarding your tattoos is that he keeps referring to them as clues of some kind. But the way he writes in the entries makes it sound more like its a hope or dream, not something he actually expects to legitimately happen." Jeffery said.

"So I'm not real?" Denis said. "This stupid tattoo isn't real? Cuz it feels real to me."

Jeffery scoffed. "Tattoos don't feel like anything unless you get them illegally done and then so, only while it heals. Don't be a wise ass."

"I'm not. My face feels like its burning."

Denis said.

Jeffery looked at his tattoo more closely. He touched it and yanked his finger back quickly, yelping.

"What the hell happened?" Denis asked, beginning to panic.

"Your face is quite hot." Jeffery said, sucking on his burnt fingers.

Denis reached out to touch his face and Jeffery stopped him, shaking his head. Denis ignored him and touched his cheek softly. He shrugged his shoulders. "It doesn't feel that hot." He said.

Confused, Jeffery touched Denis's cheek and again yelped in pain. "Jesus Christ." He shouted.

"Weird." Denis said as he kept touching his cheek.

"Painful is more like it. I wonder though."

"What?"

"What if this is a failsafe. To protect you and the tattoo from being harmed." Jeffery suggested.

"Shouldn't the rest of me be impossible to touch then?" Denis asked as he began to feel up his body. "I don't feel warm anywhere else."

Jeffery took a deep breath and reached out to touch Denis's hand. He gingerly tapped it and yanked his hand away quickly. After a moment, he touched it again. And again, until he was holding Denis's hand in his.

"Awwww, I don't usually hold hands until after the second date." Denis said.

Jeffery yanked his hand away. "You are such an ass."

"And yet you still love me." He said mockingly and Jeffery slapped his face. "Ouch. Be careful."

"Why, nothing important up there anyway." Jeffery retorted.

Denis stared at him, his mouth slack, unable for once to come up with a decent come back.

They stared each other down briefly, their eyes dancing mischievously before slumping back down and resuming their hunt for clues. They were only halfway thru the journal.

"My face hurts." Denis whined.

"Then hurry up and find all of the clues so I can figure out if I want to help your sorry ass." Jeffery said, focused on his translations.

Denis grumbled but resumed the search. The two of them sat there, going thru the fairy tale books late into the night and well into the next day.

The following day, having found all the clues that they could, Jeffery sent Denis out to check out a few sources for more fairy tale books like the ones they had disassembled already. Despite the continuous burning of the tattoo, the makeup Jeffery had made seemed to not be affected by it and held strong. However, given that it was daytime, Denis was aware that his skin had two very distinctive skin tones to it. He hugged his ball cap down as low as it could go and his hoodie pulled up, strings drawn tight and kept his face down to the ground.

The first bookstore he went into was the city's only legal bookstore. It was also the largest bookstore for underground purchases. He immediately made his way to the very back of the store and began randomly pulling out books, flipping thru their pages and returning them onto the shelving. After a few moments, the owner came to his side and asked if he could be of assistance. Denis showed him his barcode on his left wrist, similar to anyone else's, only his had an extra swirl at the one end. Slightly thicker than the rest and hardly discernible to the naked eye except for those trained to see it. The owner nodded and instructed him to follow him to the reserved section of the store. They walked around the corner, made sure no one else was in sight and opened a door that led into the back of the store. The owner pointed to a large green button and told him to push it when he was ready to make a purchase and then quickly left the hidden room.

The room immediately went pitch black as the door shut behind him. He waited a minute until his eyes began to adjust to the darkness and pulled a glow stick out of his pocket. He shook it and cracked it in the middle. A faint greenish blue light emerged from it. The room was much larger than he remembered and poorly sorted. He sighed, knowing it would take most of the day for him to sort through the jumble. He wondered if he had enough glow sticks to get him through the task.

Barely an hour later he heard the door open and the shopkeeper instructing another patron how to exit. Once he heard the door close he resumed his search, eager to get out. He had just found one of the two missing books and was excited about the possibility of finding the other one in the stacks as well. He was so focused that he never took notice of the other guest in the room or the fact that the other guest didn't have his own light source. After a few minutes his glow stick faded out completely. He felt thru his hoodie pockets, looking for another. He had just wrapped his fingers around another glow stick when he felt the cold blade of a knife pressed against his throat.

"Drop the weapon." A raspy voice said and Denis released the glow stick in his pocket.

"I'm just browsing for illegal books sir." Denis said.

The man laughed. "Don't give me that bullshit."

Denis heard the man rustling thru his own pockets followed by the glow of an already active glow stick. He held it up close to Denis's face. Out of the corner of his eye, Denis could see the man frown. He sighed with relief but only momentarily. The man moved the glow stick directly over his cheek. This guy obviously knew about the tattoo. Denis forced his breathing to remain steady and calm.

"Whatcha looking for mate. Perhaps I can help you find it." Denis offered, but the man just further pressed the blade against his throat and Denis could feel a small trickle of blood slide down.

"You know what I'm looking for. We've been searching for you for a very long time." The man said muttering. He put the glowstick in the same hand that held the knife. "No funny business or else you'll regret it." The man said as he rummaged through his pocket again.

"I'm Denis, you are?" Denis said, struggling to find a way out that didn't involve him losing his head.

"We know who you are and where you come from. We're lucky it manifested on you this time. Trying to find it in the next generation would've be tricky given your track record." The man said.

"What are you talking about?" Denis asked, genuinely confused at the man's statement. The man ignored him and produced a rag from his pocket. He began to wipe at the makeup covering the tattoo. Denis felt his heart begin to race. His secret was about to be revealed and he was at a loss at what to do. The blade was pressing further and further into his neck. Suddenly he grinned like the cat that ate the canary.

"What are you smiling about?" the man said angrily before gasping softly as the tattoo finally revealed itself.

"Beautiful isn't it?" Denis bragged. "One of a kind. It even feels pretty cool."

The man, mesmerized, let the rag drop to the ground and mesmerized, he reached out to touch it. As his fingers grazed over the tattoo he immediately let out a shriek. In that moment Denis, who had been slowly lifting his hands, reached out and grabbed the mans other hand. He pulled the knife out of his grip and pushed the man away. The man lashed out at Denis, not yet realizing that he had unknowingly relinquished his knife. Denis kicked him in the stomach and heard him fall to the ground with a thud. Still holding the knife and the fairy tale book he took off thru the stacks in the general direction of the exit.

When he ran into the wall he searched for the exit button. Denis worked his way towards where the door should have been but found only more books. It was a labyrinth of aisles of books upon books and he must have gotten turned around. The man laughed aloud.

"Can't find the exit, can we?" the man said. "Not without a little light. And when you do, I will pounce on you."

A million thoughts began to race through Denis's head. None of them helpful. Unless the owner came back with another customer he wouldn't be able to find his way out easily. So, carefully and quietly Denis worked his way along the wall, hoping to find the door purely by chance. He moved in a direction away from where he had last heard the mans' voice, knowing that it was a shot in the dark. The room was larger than the main storefront and one could easily get lost in the stacks. But he didn't know what other choice he had.

The room grew eerily quiet as the game of cat and mouse ensued. Minutes dragged on like hours when Denis felt himself suddenly fall backwards into the main part of the bookstore. The owner shook his head at him and helped pull him to his feet, scolding him for being so clumsy. Denis brushed himself off, looking around bewildered, half expecting the man to jump out of the shadows. He stumbled backwards and fell into a bookcase, causing it to teeter precariously. The owner cleared his throat and gestured to the book still in Denis's hand. Denis looked down at it and gave a smile of relief. He reached inside his jacket, pulled out a deck of cards and tossed it to the owner. The owner eyed him suspiciously as he pocketed the cards without looking at them. Denis raced out of the store with a skip in his step. The owner shook his head before showing a customer, who had been standing diligently at his side the whole time, into the secret room.

Only after he had left the store did Denis stop to realize that the new customer may have been walking into his death.

Chapter 4

When Denis got back to their apartment he found the front door torn off its hinges. Without hesitation he burst in, calling out Jeffery's name as he ran up the broken staircase. He ran straight up to their living quarters then back to the main book floor, calling out for Jeffery. It wasn't until he had reached their workshop on the top floor when he finally heard a small squeaking sound coming from one of the cabinets. He knelt down in front of it and tapped softly on it. The squeaking stopped.

"Denis?" he heard Jeffery timidly ask, his voice wavering with hope. "Is that you?" Denis forced the door open and found Jeffery squashed inside the cabinet between partitions. "Help me I'm stuck."

Denis pulled him out. "What happened here? I thought we'd talked about redecorating.

You're taste is terrible. I'm not a big fan of the messy look."

"We don't have time, we need to get out of here. Now." Jeffery said, tugging at Denis's arm.

"What happened?" Denis asked again, refusing to budge.

"They'll be back any second. When they couldn't find you I ran off and hid. Oh. Did you find another book?" He asked, his attention diverted.

Denis grabbed Jeffery by the shoulders and turned him so he could look Jeffery in the eyes. "Jeffery. Focus on me. Who was here?"

"I don't know." He stated as he took the book from Denis. "They were after you and they knew about the tattoo." Jeffery mumbled as he began flipping thru the book.

"Shit."

"What Denis, other than the obvious."

"Some guy attacked me at the bookstore. He knew about the tattoo as well."

"This can't be a coincidence. They must be working together. We need to get out of here quickly." Jeffery urged, panic rising in his voice again.

"Agreed. Where are notes? The journal?" Denis asked.

Jeffery reached into the cabinet and produced them both. "I'm not that foolish."

Denis tousled his hair, grinning as Jeffery grimaced. "I know. Lets grab what we need and get out of here."

Jeffery nodded and produced a duffel bag followed by a backpack from the cabinet. Denis shook his head, smiling at Jefferey's efficiency. Even when face with eminent danger he was always logical. Jeffery gave the duffel bag to Denis and he put the journal into the backpack before making their way downstairs. Denis disappeared off into their living quarters while Jeffery went to his books. He grabbed several books from different stacks, including the fairy tale book Denis had and a handful of glow sticks. Denis appeared from above and Jeffery waved him down. Denis dropped the duffel and jumped down into the hole landing beside Jeffery. He landed with a loud thump, clouds of dust flying up. Jeffery coughed and waved a hand in front of his face. He peeked inside the duffel bag to see it full of tools, bartering currency and what little food they had left.

Denis saw the glow sticks poking out of the backpack. "Where are we going that we'll need those?" he asked.

"Underground. Deep underground. We either go straight into the lions den or find our way beneath it." Jeffery said as he slipped the backpack on and motioned for Denis to follow him.

"Do you have connections underground that I don't?" Denis asked with surprise. Jeffery never ceased to keep surprising him despite the two of them having been joined at the hip since they were born.

The underground was very much like peeling an onion. Layer upon layer, never ending and easily able to make you cry. The government thought they knew how it operated but the truth was, so few people did. Even those running it could barely keep up with the falling down the rabbit hole adventure you knowingly took every time you stepped into its lair.

Jeffery simply nodded as he led Denis to a secret exit out of their apartment building. Denis gawked silently as he followed Jeffery under the city.

Shortly outside their apartment, only one level down, they ran smack dab into Conrad.

"Oh looky who we found. Our esteemed Private." Conrad said, his voice dripping with sugary sarcasm.

They quickly turned on their heels to walk away from Conrad and found themselves surrounded. They turned back to face Conrad.

"What do you want Lieutenant Colonel?" Denis said, letting the title roll sarcastically off of his tongue.

"Thats Sargent —" one of the soldiers said as Conrad cut him off with a stern look. The soldier slouched slightly before resuming attention.

Conrad turned to face Denis and Jeffery. "Going on a little trip, are we?"

"Awwww, you've been demoted since I last saw you." Denis smiled smugly and was rewarded with a punch to the stomach. He dropped the duffel bag and one of the soldiers picked it. He opened it, showing the contents to Conrad who quickly rifled through it.

"What, no clean underwear? How disgraceful, Private." Conrad spat out, his voice oozing with sarcasm.

"I'm just a civilian now. No need for formalities." Denis grumbled, trying to stand himself upright. Conrad punched him in the stomach again and two of the soldiers took Denis by the arms, holding him up. Jeffery stood still, his eyes darting from side to side as he tried to shrink into the shadows, afraid to move.

Conrad grabbed Denis's chin. "A civilian has much more rank than a lowly scum like you. You, who got demoted from Lieutenant Major General to Private in the blink of an eye." He turned Denis's face to the side to take a good look at his cheek. "Well what do you know? They were actually telling the truth about you." Denis glared at him with question as Conrad punched him the face, knocking him unconscious.

Jeffery stood shellshocked as he watched them dragged Denis into an unmarked van. Conrad finally acknowledged Jeffery.

"Bring him in too. He might yet prove to be useful." Conrad ordered and Jeffery let himself get dragged into the van along with Denis.

Jeffery found himself in a small room. Aside from a lone and meagre light source far above his head the room was dark. He was seated in one of two metal chairs behind a metal table. The room stank of blood, sweat, tears and death. He held his backpack in his lap, clinging nervously to it. There were no clocks or other time piece types that he could find so he was unsure how long he had been down there. Conrad had simply left him to his own devices after tossing him into the room. A quick investigation had him conclude that the mirror was a one way mirror and that the door was obviously locked. He could only sit and wait.

The door opened and Jeffery ignored it, staring absently at the mirror. Conrad stepped through the door, dragged the other metal chair across the room and sat down facing Jeffery from other side of the table. "Patient little bugger aren't you?" Conrad said. "Tell me what you know."

"That you're a malicious, ignorant asshole with the intelligence of dirt." Jeffery stated matter of fact.

Conrad clenched his fists and started to rise out of his chair. But he closed his eyes briefly before sitting back down. His commanding officer was on the other side of the mirror watching the interrogation. "Tell me about Denis."

Jeffery looked at him blankly. "Who?" he asked innocently.

"Don't play dumb with me Jeffery. Everyone here knows about the two of you. The three of us were childhood friends for chrissakes." Conrad said.

"Friends don't try to kill each other." Jeffery stated.

"I never tried to kill you. Completely." Conrad said with a laugh.

Jeffery glared at Conrad, his eyes unblinking.

"Fine, play hardball then." Conrad nodded and a bright light filled the room. The mirror became transparent and Jeffery could see Denis, on his back, strapped to a metal table. The table was raised high and the tattoo was clear for all to see. "Tell me" Conrad said, indicating the tattoo, "about that."

Jeffery looked at his friend. "Its a tattoo."

"And?"

"Its on his face?" Jeffery said.

Conrad slammed his fists into the table. "Don't play games with me Jeffery. Where did it come from?" he demanded and Jeffery shrugged his shoulders. Enraged, Conrad got to his feet, walked around the table, grabbed Jeffery by the shirt, lifted him out of his chair and slammed him into the wall. Jeffery was still clutching his backpack, his knuckles white. "Where did it come from?"

"I don't know." Jeffery said squeaking.

Conrad shook him, "Don't lie to me."

"I'm not, I swear. It just appeared on his face."

"Do you really expect me to believe that?" Conrad said, his face mere inches away from Jeffery's.

"You didn't see it the other day did you? You saw how obvious the makeup was, how could we have hidden it from you?" Jeffery said whimpering. Conrad let go of him and he slumped down to the ground.

"Makeup? Is that what you call that pasty stuff on his face?" Conrad asked and Jeffery nodded. Conrad let Jeffery fall to the ground.

"You have a valid point. For once."

Conrad knelt down beside Jeffery and looked at him sternly. "Why is the tattoo hot to the touch, but not to him? Or don't you know that either?" Jeffery shrugged his shoulders. Conrad stood up and roughly pulled Jeffery to his feet. "Look." Conrad spat in his face but Jeffery was focused on Denis. There was now several doctors in the room with him and one of them held a scalpel in his hand.

"What are you going to do to him?" Jeffery asked still looking frantically at Denis.

"What do you think? We only need the tattoo." Conrad said.

Jeffery dropped his backpack, pushed himself free of Conrad and rushed up to the glass. He pressed up against the glass and began to pound on it. He screamed at the doctor to stop. Conrad pulled him off of the glass and shoved Jeffery down into the chair. "Behave yourself or I'll have you removed." He ordered.

"You don't want to do this. You'll get hurt." Jeffery insisted.

"Don't feed me that bullshit. You admitted that you know nothing about the tattoo." Conrad said, shrugging his shoulders and indicating that the doctor should continue.

Jeffery jumped to his feet and grabbed Conrad's arm. Conrad brushed him off.

"Please don't. You don't know what will happen." Jeffery pleaded.

"And neither do you. Now sit down, shut up and watch your friend die." Conrad barked at him as the doctor began his first incision.

As soon as the blade touched the skin around the tattoo the doctor was flung against the mirror by an invisible source. The scalpel was buried deep into his throat and the doctor gurgled as he quickly bled to death, his skin melting off of his face like ice cream on a hot summer day. The other doctors stepped away from Denis, their eyes wide with disbelief. One of them shouted out, pointed at Denis's face as a green, almost transparent gas, emanated from his tattoo. The doctor closet to Denis suddenly gripped his throat, gasping for air. The other doctors ran for the door only to find it locked. They cried out for the room to be flushed out and to open the door. But it remained locked and the air in the room remained still. One by one, they struggled for air and died a quick yet painful death from asphyxiation. When the last doctors had taken their final breath the air suddenly came to life in the room and the gas was quickly swept out by the ventilation system. The locked door popped open.

Denis's eyes fluttered. He tried to sit up but found himself strapped down. He called out to

Conrad and Jeffery, asking where they were. Conrad stood just as shellshocked as Jeffery.

Gathering what courage he could muster, Jeffery stood up behind Conrad. "I told you not to do that." Conrad slowly turned around, his face twitching as he looked at Jeffery. "I never said that I didn't know anything about the tattoo. Didn't I?" Conrad looked back at the room where Denis was strapped down and then back at Jefferey.

"You." Conrad managed to mutter.

"I need to talk. But not to you." Jeffery said. "Now let him go."

Chapter 5

Denis was sitting on a couch in a fresh change of clothes. He had woken up strapped to a table when Jeffery had appeared. In the few moments that they were alone Jeffery tried to explain what had happened, but soldiers rushed into the room and dragged the two of them out in separate directions. Denis was led to a shower facility and had the luxury of an actual hot shower for the first time in his life. The closest he had ever had to that before was when his parental units would heat up the bath water, put it in a container and sprinkle it over his head. That seemed like a lifetime ago.

Denis stepped out of the shower to find clean clothes laid out on a bench. Relatively new jeans, slightly faded, a white T-shirt with some band logo strewn across the front and a black leather jacket already broken in. He smiled as he saw the faded converse on the floor beneath the bench. It was like someone had raided his own closet. There was also a large spread of food on a rolling table before him. He slowly got dressed then ate. He laid down on the couch, expecting only to get comfortable but quickly found himself falling asleep.

He awoke later to find Conrad, disgruntled and annoyed, in front of the couch, asking Denis to come with him. With a smug smile on his face Denis jumped to his feet and followed Conrad out the door. As they walked down the corridor, Conrad remained silent but visibly upset. Denis could not help but gloat at his old friends change of attitude.

"Whats the matter friend, cat got your tongue?" Denis chuckled as he slapped Conrad across the shoulders. Conrad managed an angry glare at Denis then looked away as he turned the corner sharply. "Aww c'mon. We used to be friends. Here," Denis said, taking Conrad's hand and bringing it close to his face, "wanna touch it?"

Conrad yanked his hand free and plastered himself against the wall, sheer terror in his eyes. Denis took a step back and looked at Conrad carefully. "Sheesh, I don't want to kill you." He said, with no emotion in his voice.

The door beside Conrad opened up and Denis

walked through it shaking his head. A voice from inside bellowed and Conrad rushed into the room.

Inside the room sat Jeffery, as squeaky clean as Denis, the Major General and the head of the current government. Denis was already sitting down beside Jeffery when Conrad stumbled in and stood to the side at full attention. The Major General waved, indicating that Conrad join them at the table. Conrad timidly sat down.

They sat like this for several moments before the Major General cleared his throat.

"Private Roy," The Major General started and Denis cut him off.

"Sir, I'm no longer with the service. I'm just a civilian now. Call me Denis, please." He said softly.

The Major General eyed him suspiciously but continued. "Alright, Mr. Roy. It has been brought to our attention that you have something we desire to possess. Despite our attempts to obtain this in a humane—" Jeffery interrupted him by coughing loudly and the Major General raised an eyebrow in annoyance before continuing. "— we have discovered that in order to get what we desire, we require you alive. Unfortunately."

"Sorry." Denis said shrugging his shoulders unapologetically.

"So. We would like to make a proposal. You help us and we'll help you." The Major General stated.

"And why, exactly would I want to help you?" Denis said leaning back in his seat, his voice icy.

The Major General motioned towards Jeffery. Denis looked questioningly from the Major General to Jeffery.

"Jeffery?" Denis asked carefully, giving his friend the chance to indicate if whatever was about to pass thru his lips was a lie or a ruse. But Jeffery looked too excited for Denis to know which.

"The Major General is in possession of some old journals. Written in gibberish." Jeffery said with a smile and Denis laughed out loud. Conrad and the Major General looked at each other suspiciously. "The journals, although only partially translated, contain a lot more information than I expected. It turns out that the doctor had an assistant, who also kept meticulous records of their research and projects." Jeffery said, fidgeting anxiously in his seat.

"Get to the point Jeffery." Denis said.

"The tattoos are clues. Like a scavenger hunt or a treasure map. You need to figure out where the clue leads too in order to trigger the next clue. If you don't do that within a specific time frame after the tattoo first appears then. Um. It will consume you." Jeffery said in a spurt.

Denis softly touched the tattoo and realized that it was actually slightly painful to his touch now. Jeffery nodded his head slowly. Denis stared Jeffery squarely in the eye and glanced slightly in the direction of the backpack and then at the Major General. Jeffery shrugged his shoulders.

"Gentlemen." the Major General said firmly.

"Gibberish?" Denis asked and Jeffery nodded.

Conrad looked thoroughly confused, the Major General looked impatient and the government leader looked bored. The conversation at hand was above his pay grade and his presence was nothing more than a formality.

"What exactly do you propose then? What's in it for us?" Denis asked.

Conrad began to rise from his seat in anger but the Major General waved him down. "We will help you figure out where the clue leads, take you to the clue and so forth until we reach the end." The Major General said.

"What's at the end? What do you get out of it?" Denis asked skeptically.

"Global domination." The Major General stated matter as fact0.

"Wow." Denis said, unsure of what else to say. "You cut straight to the chase didn't you?"

"We're not the only faction interested in you Mr. Roy. There's no need to beat around the bush. If another faction gets ahold of you, they're likely going to sugar coat the truth. No point since your friend here will most likely figure it out on his own eventually. Given that he's the only one who appears to be able to translate this 'gibberish'. Even with the limited resources that you may have access to."

"So what do we get out of it?" Denis asked.

"Simply put, you get to live. Because if you refuse we will kill you and then simply wait for the tattoo to manifest onto someone else." The Major General said as he got out of his chair. "But a man like you isn't afraid of death. So that isn't much of a bargaining chip, is it? Despite your recent activities, I know that you are a man of honour and respect, who wants to do good by humanity. You never meant to get involved in the events that led to your dishonourable discharge. You're a good man, aren't you?" By now the Major General was standing behind him. He leaned over Denis's shoulder so he could address them both. "Let us help you and you will get the chance to save humanity." He whispered softly then stood back up.

Denis looked at Jeffery with question. Jeffery

slowly nodded his head. Denis looked at the Major General. "What makes you think this tattoo will help save humanity? What proof do you have?" Denis asked.

The Major General looked at Jeffery who wriggled uncomfortably in his seat. "They have several journals from the doctors assistant, documenting the entire project from beginning to end. Complete with drawings and meticulous details."

"So, why do you even need me? Not that I don't want to be the hero." Denis asked.

"Why must you always resist?" Conrad said shouting at him.

"Sargent." The Major General said firmly and Conrad begrudgingly sat down.

Jeffery continued. "Their journals are not translated. They only recently found a translator and have barely begun to scratch the surface on it. Their translator is more guessing then knowing. What I managed to translate in the little time they let me see the journal is that the tattoos are, like I said, clues. Each tattoo will lead to a new clue which triggers a new tattoo. Until you reach the last clue and then find the prize. Which is apparently a device that will save humanity."

"Sir, how do we even know that this device exists? Wasn't the doctor killed?" Conrad asked angrily.

"What doctor?" Denis asked.

"Doctor Fredrickson."   The Major General said.

"Dr. Fredrickson….. Why does that name sound familiar?" Denis asked himself softly. Jeffery looked at him puzzled.

"He was the scientist, the real scientist, that came up with the toxin that made us how we are now." Jeffery said quietly.

"But the history books said it was—" Denis started.

"The history books say what we want you to know.   Dr. Fredrickson had defected.   He was working on a secret project the whole time he was supposed to be improving the toxin.   Until recently, we had presumed he was working on a weapon to destroy humanity.   We now believe this to be incorrect." The Major General declared, almost proud of the fact that they had the power to lie so easily.

"Jeffery." Denis said softly, as he held gaze and locked eyes with the Major General.   "Do you think this project can really save us all?   Or do you think its a weapon to kills us all."

Without a moments hesitation Jeffery simply said. "Life."

Denis smiled and the Major General took his seat across from them again. "He stays with me." Denis said indication Jeffery.

"Impossible." The Major General said. "We only need you. We can assure you that no harm will come to him though."

"Thats bullshit and you know it. The second he's out of my sight you'll kill him. I have no way of communicating with him after he leaves. Besides, he's the best translator in the world. If you had even half a brain you would have scouted him out the second you got the journals." Denis said firmly.

"They already have, they just don't know it." Jeffery said timidly.

"What?" Conrad said angrily, "Thats complete and utter —" but the Major General cut him off with the wave of a hand and looked at Jeffery.

Jeffery took a deep breath and exhaled slowly. "Some of the black market translations I have done this past year have been part of the journal. I recognize the handwriting. Alone, a single page doesn't translate to much. Not enough to trigger concern. But when you showed me the journal you had today, even as incomplete as the copy you were showing me was, I recognized it."

The Major General turned to face Conrad. "Sargent, or should I now say Lieutenant Colonel? How exactly did this gentlemen come across top secret military documents? Did you really resort to black market translators?" he demanded. Conrad began to flush a bright deep red and his words began to stammer out of his mouth as he admitted something along the lines of sourcing out the translation.

Denis looked over at Jeffery and whispered, "I had always wondered why he left you alone."

Jeffery shrugged his shoulders with a small smile. "I have copies." He said softly to Denis.

Thoroughly embarrassed Conrad sat meekly in his chair beside the Major General trying to grow smaller. He hadn't even realized that despite his anger the Major General had given him a promotion in rank. The Major General turned back to face Denis and Jeffery with a fake smile plastered on his face. The anger beneath it dangerously visible. "It seems, gentlemen, that we have an agreement. Jeffery will join the research team that is currently attempting to decipher the location of the the first clue." The Major General started.

"I think I have an idea of where it is." Jeffery said, eagerly interrupting him.

The Major General growled under his breath. "Conrad. Why don't you escort Jeffery to the other researchers so they can ascertain if his location is accurate or not. Following that, get everyone to prepare for departure. I want us to move out by 0600. Time is a delicacy we don't have. Isn't that correct?" he said, looking directly at Jeffery who was now wearing the smuggest of smiles.

Conrad stood up and indicated for Jeffery to follow him. Jeffery followed him out the door. Once shut the Major General glared at sternly Denis. "I don't want any shenanigans or trouble on this mission. Do we have an understanding, Private?" the Major General said, emphasizing the word 'private'.

Denis stopped himself from correcting the Major General and with an equally hard gaze he simply said, "Understood."

As they boarded the plane Jeffery was unable to contain his excitement. It was his first time in a plane and he very much resembled a five year old. Like the first time his parental units had given him candy. Back when his parents still loved him. Denis, on the other hand, could barely keep himself awake and laid his head down on Jeffery's lap as they sat down.

"Haven't changed much have you?" Conrad said shaking his head while Denis flipped him the bird. Jeffery buckled Denis in first then himself before pulling out his files and setting them on Denis's head.

"You are a cruel man Jeffery." Denis

mumbled, swatting at the files.

"Go to sleep. I'll wake you up once we reach our destination." Jeffery said ignoring him as Denis grumbled something about cruel and unusual punishment for a hero before falling asleep.

The Major General boarded the plane, as did several other military personnel. They ignored Denis as they gathered around Jeffery. His thoughts on the location had turned out to be correct. The military researchers were hampered by their lack of knowledge of the earths geography in the past. Due to a mixture of the loss of technology, time passing and the last big war, the number of accurate geographical and historical books lost was astronomical. As a result, the military was grossly misinformed of the past. Something that until now, had never been an issue. Jeffery's immense book collection was surpassed only by his photographic memory. Both he and the researchers had determined that the tattoo could be directly translated into longitude and latitude, but they had disagreed on where. They had thought it would have in located in Sector B, which was once known as Kazakhstan, whereas Jeffery thought it was located in Sector D, also known as Iceland. They had fought all through the night until Jeffery had finally drawn up a map, from memory, of earth at the time of Dr. Fredrickson's existence. When they laid that map over the one they had of earth currently they realized that Sector B and D overlapped each other.

Given this new information the researchers begrudgingly agreed that Jeffery may actually be correct and therefore they were en route to Sector D. Also known as Sector Death. The residents of that sector had died out years ago. The cause of their death unknown. The government had simply deemed the island quarantined and no one had set foot on it since.

As the plane took off Jeffery got giddy, his eyes glued to the small window beside him. He watched in awe as they levelled out in the sky. Once the flight was underway Jeffery turned his attention to the documents in front of him. Denis yawned and stretched, knocking the papers to the ground. Jeffery grumbled as Denis sat up, rubbing the sleep out of his eyes. He helped Jeffery gather up his paperwork and undid his seatbelt at the same time. Once Jeffery was settled back into his chair he resumed reading the journal entries; page by page. An empty notebook sat beside him the pencil laying in its middle.

Denis leaned over glancing at the entries. "Are those the ones they gave you?" he asked softly and Jeffery nodded. "You should write down what you read, before you forget it." He said softly, looking over the chair at the other researchers around them who were straining to listen to their conversation.

"But I—" Jeffery started.

"Have a terrible memory, yes I know." Denis finished for him. Jeffery went to protest but stopped himself just as quickly.

"You're right. I'm good with remembering pictures, but that's pretty much it." Jeffery confirmed.

"Yup. Too bad the journal's not a picture book huh?" Denis said with a laugh as he slapped Jeffery on the shoulders.

Jeffery began to jot down notes directly into the journal. He began to translate the words literally, so they would make less sense then they should and adding an occasional notation of gibberish. Denis smiled and got out of his seat.

"So what does a man have to do to get a little in flight service?" he asked mischievously.

Their plane had long since landed and the team dispersed. Jeffery and Denis were leading the way with Conrad, the Major General and a small group of personnel. The researchers had remained on the plane. They had no way knowing if Sector D was in fact void of life. The last update was from well over a hundred years ago. If anyone or anything had survived they would be at risk. The Major General knew this when he had decided to follow them, but he had to see first hand what would happen when they found the first location. The researchers had felt that there would be a device of some kind that the tattoo would trigger while Jeffery remained skeptical. The vague description in the journal led him to believe that Dr. Fredrickson had never really tested as much as he had theorized.

The hangar bay that they had landed in was eerily empty. No decayed corpses or remains of any kind to be seen. The air was void of life and they found it difficult to breath. They kept themselves at a slow yet steady pace to prevent the overuse of what little oxygen was in the air. Denis was leading the way mostly by instinct at this point. As soon as they had landed his tattoo had begun to glow and pulse softly. He couldn't explain it, but he equated it to the equivalent of playing a game of hot or cold. He felt his face get painfully warm as they had landed so he presumed the more it hurt, the closer they were getting and vice versa.

The Major General had been quite excited at this change despite his usual gruff demeanour. He had also seemed unsurprised. Jeffery inquired to the amount of pain Denis was in. Denis laughed and said it was enough that he might just take a scalpel to his face himself if they didn't find the next clue soon enough. Jeffery tried to laugh it off with him, but the quiver in Denis's hand said he wasn't lying. The Major General grew quiet during their exchange.

They made their way thru the ghost ships and into a corridor. Despite the lack of life, there seemed to be a sufficient amount of electrical power running through the station. The lights were on, the doors slid open automatically and a voice occasionally chirped out their location as they entered a new room.

"This sector is quite advanced compared to ours isn't it?" Jeffery said aloud.

"Makes you wonder what could have killed them?" Conrad said snidely.

"Kill? I thought they died mysteriously?" Jeffery said.

"They did." Conrad started. "But don't you think that if it was some kind of illness that they would have at least tried to send out a transmission to the other sectors warning them away?"

Jeffery stopped short, realizing the validity of Conrad's point.

"Regardless of whatever killed them, it was

so long ago that I doubt it is still here." Denis said, grumbling. "Otherwise, wouldn't they have sent out a proper welcoming committee?"

"Perhaps, they're waiting to take us out, one by one." Conrad said. "Lurking about the shadows."

Jeffery shivered at the thought and Denis slugged him in the shoulder. "Ignore that dumbass. He was always good at getting under your skin." Denis muttered. Jeffery nodded in agreement but stuck his tongue out at Conrad before following Denis.

Denis turned down a corridor triggering the opening of a hidden door. A voice chirped out telling them that they were entering the cafeteria. Denis broke out in a trot, "Woowee! Maybe I can finally get me some decent grub." He called out as he disappeared around the corner.

"Denis, stay in sight." Conrad barked as Jeffery shrugged his shoulders with a half smile at Denis's antics. His lack of care had always irked Conrad when they were kids and it made Jeffery laugh that it still did years later.

Conrad picked up his pace, jogged past Jeffery and around the corner. He cursed loudly and Jeffery rolled his eyes at the Major General, who only grunted. They rounded the corner into the cafeteria, which was surprisingly neat and tidy despite a potential mass execution or sector wide epidemic. It was also completely empty aside from Conrad.

"Denis?" Jeffery called out but no one answered.

Conrad began to spew profanities as he dispersed the remaining troops to begin a search for Denis. The Major General barked at Conrad to find him then turned his attention to Jeffery.

"Do you have any idea where he would have disappeared too?" the Major General barked. Jeffery could only shake his head. "You had better hope, for your sake, that he reappears quickly." The Major General said as he slide his hand into his jacket to reveal a concealed handgun.

Chapter 6

Denis rubbed his head gingerly. He had ran around the corner quickly hoping to piss off Conrad only to be rewarded with a blow to his head. As he tried to get to his feet someone pushed down to the ground. A gruff voice told him to sit down and be quiet. He complied, mostly out of surprise. Denis was certain that he had heard that voice before, but he couldn't quite place it.

Several muffled voices could be heard in the dark surrounding him. As well, he could hear Jeffery calling out for him as a blade pressed firmly against his throat. Moments later he heard someone say that the area was clear and he was pulled to his feet. They pulled his arms pulled in front and tied his hands together while another person pulled a gag over his mouth. His tattoo immediately burned thru the gag and their hand. Denis laughed loudly. He was rewarded with a slap to the other side of his face as the gruff voice again told him to shut it.

A door opened and light poured in. One of the men scanned the cafeteria before pulling Denis out of the closet they were hiding in. Out in the open he recognized the man with the gruff voice. It was the customer he thought he had sent to his death in the bookstore. The man had barely spoken two words, but Denis recognized the gruffness of his voice. It sounded like his vocal cords had once been ripped out and then forcibly put back. As if to prove this theory the man had a large scar on his throat. The man saw Denis eyeing his throat and gave a sinister smile as he yanked Denis along by the arm.

They led Denis thru the cafeteria and back out into the main corridor. They led towards the docking area only to stop in front of a series of bookcases built into the wall. They pulled on a book and the bookcase slide away from the wall. Denis felt his tattoo flare up, burning thru the gag.

"Holy shit." Denis murmured and they all turned to look at his cheek, now a vibrant bright red. The gag smouldering on the floor at his feet.

"C'mon, hurry up. Before the others find us.

Block the path and stand guard. We shouldn't be long." The man with the gruff voice said.

"Where are you taking me?" Denis asked dumbly.

"To Disneyland of course." The man with the gruff voice said and the others laughed.

"Do you have a name?" Denis said trying to stall them.

The man stopped and looked at Denis suspiciously. "I can't tell if you're trying to be a smart ass or if you're genuinely sincere. But, you don't strike me as an overly intelligent man," He said, gauging Denis for a reaction. "My name's Chuck." He pulled Denis further into the hidden room.

"Do I get to ride the roller coaster Chuck?" Denis asked smugly.

"Sort of. Providing that it doesn't kill you first." Chuck said with a laugh.

Denis stopped abruptly. "Kill me? Really? Wouldn't it defeat the purpose of finding this treasure if it kills me?"

Chuck laughed. "They're really keeping the two of you in the dark, aren't they?"

"What are you talking about?" Denis asked.

"Yes, each clue leads to a device that triggers the next clue. Which is technically your mysteriously appearing tattoo." Chuck paused as Denis nodded slowly. "But this isn't the first that time they've been here. Its their second time. The first time they thought they had the right person. Unfortunately, their mistake resulted in that person's death. Haven't you wondered why the place seems so void of anything? So sterile?"

"But why let me lead them the wrong way?" Denis asked.

"If they knew the way wouldn't it arouse your suspicion? Better to let you think that you 'found it' all on your own." Chuck said.

"How come I didn't sense this area?" Denis asked.

"Lead bookcases. Blocks the signal." Chuck said pulling him along.

"How did you know that if the others were fakes?"

"You're not the only ones with a translator." Chuck said smugly. "This way. We're almost there."

Denis stopped again.

"What?" asked Chuck.

"I'm scared." Denis admitted.

"Of what? Dying?" Chuck said. "A big boy like you?" he laughed.

Denis began to step backwards, his eyes growing wide and nodded. The man behind grabbed Denis by the shoulders and turned Denis to face him. Denis's lips were trembling and his eyes frantic. The man sighed and in that moment Denis grabbed the man's head, pressing his tattoo against the man's face. He screamed as he spontaneously burst into flames. Denis stepped away from the man, holding his still tied up hands to the tattoo. The smell of smoke filled his nostrils as the tattoo quickly burned thru the rope. Chuck yelled at his men to capture Denis but they hesitated, their companion still screaming in his death throes. Denis grinned and ran back down the corridor towards the main entrance. Chuck screamed at his men and pursued Denis on his own.

Denis retraced his steps back but darted into a different corridor then the one they came thru. He quickly ducked down as he heard Chuck's angry voice approaching. He watched as Chuck ran right past where he was hiding. Denis contemplated following Chuck to try and take him out by surprise, but thought better and continued down the corridor.

A few moments later he bumped into Jeffery, knocking the two of them down to the ground. Denis's face accidentally brushed Jeffery's hand and Jeffery grimaced in pain. Denis immediately apologized as he helped Jeffery to his feet.

"Where did you go?" Jeffery demanded angrily.

"Hey, hey, hey. Why the anger? I'm still here." Denis said.

"Yeah, but I almost wasn't. The Major General was ready to kill me as soon as you disappeared." Jeffery grumbled.

"But you're okay now."

"No thanks to you." Jeffery retorted.

Denis sighed. "It wasn't my fault. I was ambushed as soon as I went into the cafeteria. They were waiting for us."

"Who was waiting for you? Santa Claus?" Jeffery retorted.

Denis held up his wrists so Jeffery could see the burn marks on them. "Santa Claus isn't real. These guys are. I think they're the same guys that tried to capture me in the bookstore and probably ransacked our place." Denis said. "C'mon. We need to hide out for a moment while I think things through." Denis went to run further down the corridor, but Jeffery took him by the arm and led him down another corridor. They walked into a large medical bay. Jeffery then led him into a closet.

"How the heck did you find this?" Denis asked.

Jeffery smiled slyly. "When one is not as strong as you are, you have to make up by being sneaky."

Denis laughed and slapped him on the

shoulder. "Good job mate. Now how the hell do we get out of here?"

"We need to find the device and trigger your next tattoo. But first, there's something I need to tell you. I read about something on the plane that might interest you." Jeffery said his voice becoming a hushed whisper.

"Not now. We need to get out of this alive first. And I think I know where the device is." Denis said.

"Really? Why haven't you gone to it yet?" Jeffery demanded.

"And let you miss out on all the fun?" Denis said with a smile. "We need to get back downstairs. The other faction had me below deck level. There weren't any windows but we only went down a single flight of stairs."

"This way." Jeffery said stepping aside to reveal a door at the far back of the closet.

"Seriously? Are you sure you aren't the mad scientist?" Denis asked him flabbergasted.

Jeffery rolled his eyes. "Please. Don't give me that much credit. Dr. Fredrickson was brilliant." He sighed softly, his eyes filled with admiration. Denis tousled his hair. "When I hid from the Major General I ran into this room. The door doesn't lock so I was trying to hide myself amongst the supplies when I found the passageway by mistake. Someone must have designed it for emergencies."

"Interesting. Alright. Lead the way." Denis said.

Jeffery stepped thru and Denis closed the door behind them. As soon as the door closed the passageway filled with darkness. Then a low glow flickered above, filling the passage way as their eyes adjusted. Denis nodded his head with approval as they descended down the stairs.

When they emerged from the staircase they found themselves in what looked like the exact same room that they had been in only moments ago. Denis looked around murmuring something about too much weirdness in this building. Denis felt his cheek flare up and wave for Jeffery to follow him.

Jeffery abruptly grabbed Denis by the arm and pulled on it hard. Denis looked back at him, anger on his face.

"What?" Denis snarled.

"There's something you need to know Denis. Its important." Jeffery insisted.

"More important than finding the device and not dying in the process because we now have two factions interested in me?" he asked pulling away from Jeffery.

"Yes." Jeffery demanded, pulling on his arm so hard that Denis fell backwards onto him.

"Christ Jeffery, you trying to get yourself killed? My tattoo is a bit on the dangerous side right now."

"So is this device." Jeffery started.

"I already know." Denis said. Jeffery looked at him surprised. "Chuck told me."

"Chuck? Who's Chuck?" Jeffery asked.

" I think he's the leader of that other faction. He told me that this isn't the government's first time here. They've brought someone else and they died trying to trigger the device." Denis said trying to scout out the area.

"That explains why it didn't take much effort to convince them I was right about the location." Jeffery mumbled to himself. Denis went to stand back up but Jeffery pulled him back down "There's more to it." He said quickly. "Its why you can die."

"Isn't obvious, you can't fake the tattoos." Denis said, but Jeffery shook his head. "Then what?"

"When they first released the toxin into our atmosphere only Dr. Fredrickson, his assistant, select members of the government and their families were immune to it." Jeffery started, his voice suddenly growing quiet. They heard the sounds of footsteps drawing closer to their location and Denis slowly stood up. Jeffery held his breath as the footsteps kept getting closer only to change direction away from them. Once he was sure that they had receded completely Denis knelt back down beside Jeffery.

"Whats the big deal then? That makes sense, doesn't it? You wouldn't want to risk your own family." Denis said.

"But when he died, Dr. Fredrickson had a wife and child." Jeffery said.

"So. . . " Denis started and stopped as it sunk in. "You can't undo the toxin's affect can you?" he asked, already knowing the answer. The government was like royalty. You could never work your way into it. It was the only profession that you had to be born into. No one ever got assigned by chance into the government. The military was another story altogether.

"How do you guarantee that the biological key will even emerge?" Jeffery asked.

"You alter one of the unaffected. You adapt them to become the key. You alter them in such a way that the genetics required to trigger the device would always be passed down." Denis said absently. "Holy shit."

"Yeah. Holy shit is right. Only its your shit that's holy." Jeffery said.

"Do they know?" Denis asked.

Jeffery shook his head. "I translated this from the notes that we found in the fairy tale books. Dr. Fredrickson's grief and anger came from falling in love with someone who couldn't escape the fate that he had created. He had forced himself upon her. She eventually succumbed to him, perhaps even loving him, but he felt guilty about it none the less. When his child was conceived he knew he had to take opportunity of genetics that were still alterable."

"But the other person, they must have had a tattoo that appeared like mine did. Why would theirs not trigger the device?" Denis asked, worried.

"They probably have to be a direct descendant or maybe their blood must have been impure." Jeffery speculated.

"Am I a direct descendant?" Denis asked hopefully.

Jeffery shrugged his shoulders. "No one has kept track of lineage outside of the government families. There's no way to know."

"Well, there's one way to find out." Denis said standing up.

"You can't. You might die." Jeffery said, trying to pull him back down.

"What choice do I have Jeffery? The only way the two of us leave this sector alive, is if we find the device, trigger it and I live. Otherwise, we're sitting ducks." Denis stated. "Besides didn't you say the tattoo would consume me otherwise?"

Jeffery sighed, knowing that Denis was right. He stood up. "Come with me."

Denis followed him without hesitation. "Where are we going?"

"To the device." Jeffery said.

Denis grabbed Jeffery's arm. "You know where it is?"

"I always have. I memorized the old blueprints of the sector and deduced from it the most logical location for the device to be hidden." Jeffery said.

"And you're only telling me this now?" Denis said, annoyed.

"When you were busy being a jackass on the flight I translated the stuff about you needing to be a direct descendant. I had always intended to lead the way when we got here, but I was curious as to how the tattoo would react being this close to the device. I wanted to find a way to make them think I was wrong and that the device was in Sector B, not D, but it was too late." Jeffery said, hanging his head low. "I messed up."

"No, no, no Jeffery. You did great. I'm the one who's sorry. I messed up. I shouldn't have gone along with the search for the device so easily. Now, we don't have a choice. So lets get this over with." Denis said grimly as the two of them walked down the corridor together.

As Denis and Jeffery stepped into the room where the device was they weren't surprised to find Conrad, the Major General, and Chuck waiting inside. The two groups were armed to the teeth, weapons pointed at each others. Denis looked between the two groups and sighed heavily.

"What, no hello? No welcome back? No, go ahead and please don't die this time?" Denis said haughtily.

Conrad looked genuinely surprised while the Major General just looked annoyed. Chuck feigned innocence as he shrugged his shoulders.

Jeffery and Denis walked thru and stopped in the middle of their weapons.

Jeffery waved his hands in front of them. "Please, you're blocking the way." He said as rudely as possible.

Denis smiled brightly. Moments like these, where Jeffery's 'inner beast' came out always made him so proud. The two groups parted like Moses parted the red sea. Both Denis and Jeffery walked through to the console that lay beyond them.

"Okay, now what?" Denis asked Jeffery.

"I dunno. I hadn't gotten that far in the translations. Gimmie a sec." Jeffery said, flipping through the journal that he held in his hands. He hemmed and hawed while Denis looked at both Chuck and the Major General expectantly.

"Hello, gentlemen? You've both been here before, haven't you? What did the guy before me do?" Denis asked.

The Major General shrugged his shoulders and Chuck rolled his eyes. "Christ, really? You're going to pretend that you don't know anything? He already knows that you're lying to him. I may have been here then but I wasn't close enough to see what he did." Chuck admitted.

"She did." The Major General corrected before realizing his error. The Major General walked over to the console and pressed a sequence of buttons. A scanner lifted out of the console. "Just hold your face up to it and let the scanner do its thing." He said as he quickly stepped away from the console. Chuck and the others also took a few more cautious steps back.

Denis looked at his friend. "You're more than welcome to join them. I think I may be about to spontaneously combust."

Jeffery shook his head. "I'd rather die accidentally by your hand than intentionally by theirs. They're more likely to keep me alive and torture me as they force me to translate the journals."

Denis nodded in agreement and took Jeffery's hand in his as he leaned towards the scanner. It immediately chirped to life. Denis trembled slightly and clenched his eyes shut. The others, hidden in the outer reaches of the room, watched as the scanner emitted a red laser that scanned the entirety of his tattoo. The laser disappeared as it chirped again and his tattoo faded away. Jeffery gasped and let go of Denis's hand. With his eyes still closed Denis asked if everything was alright. Jeffery nodded. Chuck snorted and Denis slowly opened his eyes.

"I'm not dead?" Denis asked. Jeffery, unable to speak, just pointed to his cheek. Denis touched his cheek. "Is it gone?" he asked and again Jeffery nodded. "Did it work? Is there another tattoo?"

Jeffery shook his head from side to side before he began to examine Denis more closely. But couldn't find anything. The others were still too afraid to get any closer and watched as Denis stripped down to his skivvies and Jeffery thoroughly examined him. Jeffery pulled the back of Denis's underwear away from his body and shook his head. Denis looked down the front of his underwear and also shook his head.

Denis redressed and Chuck grumbled about needing the next clue and how they must have fucked something up. He and the Major General began to argue with each other.

Jeffery, ignoring them, began to start pushing buttons on the console. Denis asked him if it was a smart idea to do that.

"They missed something in their notes. Dr. Fredrickson was brilliant. He would leave nothing to chance. Nor would he make it too simple. First step was acknowledging the proper heritage." Jeffery hissed as he continued to input what appeared to be random data into the console. The two groups had resumed holding weapons at each other while arguing over who had messed things up.

"What are doing to the console?" Conrad asked, finally taking notice. The Major General and Chuck stopped their arguing long enough to look at what Jeffery was doing. The three of them began to step further away from the console, fear dancing in their eyes.

"Answer the man." The Major General ordered.

"Answering it." Jeffery said.

"I said to answer the man." The Major General said again.

Jeffery stopped what he doing and looked up at the Major General. "And I did. I am answering it.   The console is asking us questions."

They looked at Jeffery dumbly.

"It wants to know who Denis is. I'm just inputing his birthdate and parental units information.   Nothing more." He resumed inputting the data. A few seconds later a hole appeared in the device. "Put your right hand in." He instructed Denis. Denis did as he was told and the others jumped further back seeking shelter. Nothing happened. Jeffery looked at the console and then the journal. "Sorry, put your left hand in." Denis shrugged, removed his right hand and put his left hand in.

The console immediately gripped his hand and sucked his whole arm in. Denis lurched forward, his face smacking into the console. He swore, accusing the console of trying to rip his arm off. While this happened, no one noticed the console spitting out a slew of paper. Jeffery grabbed it and shoved into his satchel. As soon as he did the console let go of Denis's arm. He pulled his arm out and winced as he rubbed his arm.

"Are you okay?" Jeffery asked and Denis nodded his head. As he did a new tattoo appeared on his face. This one looked like a cockroach. The one non humanoid life form that had survived all the wars and devastation humanity had thrust upon the earth. Denis touched his cheek as the tattoo emerged.

"Why is my tattoo moving." Denis asked hesitantly.

"Uhhh." Jeffery started, unable to complete his sentence as he stared at the wriggling cockroach on Denis's face.

"I think this one is alive." Conrad said, his face grimacing with disgust. Even the Major General couldn't maintain his composure.

"Jeffery?" Denis said, turning to face his friend who proceeded to jump out of his skin. "What the hell is on my face?"

"I think. I think." Jeffery said stuttering.

Denis grabbed Jeffery's hand and pulled it close to his face. Jeffery squealed like a girl. "Tell me what it is or I'm going to make you touch it." He threatened.

"A cockroach. Oh my god, its a cockroach." Jeffery cried out and Denis let go of his hand. Jeffery fell to the floor with tears in his eyes.

"Fuck me." Denis said.

Conrad laughed, "Ain't nobody gonna fuck you now with that on your face."

Denis charged over and punched Conrad in the face before he had a chance to react. Conrad tried to fight back but he was too busy laughing to do much more than fend off Denis's fists as they flew at him. Finally the Major General whistled and they both immediately ceased fighting. The Major General ordered them to their feet and they both stood up. Conrad took a large step away from Denis as he did.

"Um, Denis." Jeffery said, his voice a mere whisper.

"What?" Denis said angrily.

"Where did Chuck go?" Jeffery asked and they all looked around the room to see that Chuck and his faction had disappeared.

Chapter 7

Back at base Jeffery and the researchers were busy trying to decipher how a cockroach related to the next location.   Cockroaches were, unfortunately for them, a life form that had at one point, existed everywhere on the entire planet. They were the only other life form, aside from humans, that had survived the great wars. Those that had survived though, were plagued with radiation and burrowed deep beneath the planets surface.

Whenever he had a moment to himself, Jeffery would sneak out the papers the first device had given him. After Denis had been scanned, Jeffery had the crazy idea to type in Dr. Fredrickson's word 'HELP' into the console. He had hoped that Dr. Fredrickson had built in failsafes to help prevent the devices from falling into the wrong hands. From the moment Jeffery had realized that the tattoos would trigger some type of life saving device he felt that there had to be more to it. Much more. Why else would Dr. Fredrickson hide a device that would help save humanity?

Was the government so corrupt back then that they wouldn't have wanted to save everyone? If the present government was right in their assumption then the device would allow whomever triggered it to have full control of the planet. However, since Dr. Fredrickson had already given the government full control of the toxins with the scanning technology, why didn't he just hand over the device over willingly? Why be so secretive? Jeffery knew he was missing a vital piece to the puzzle and he had to find it before they reached the final device.

When he had typed 'HELP' into the console it had replied with 'WHY'. His heart had leapt into his throat and he had almost lost his composure. He managed to keep himself clearheaded, knowing that the others would only be distracted for so long. Jeffery had then engaged in a conversation with the console, telling it that they had been captured by the enemy and forced to comply. When it gave him the option to kill them all or to save humanity, he had chosen to save humanity. When the console had asked him why, he had told it that it was worth the risk. Obviously satisfied with his answer the console said it would provide a distraction. That was when it spit out a slew of papers in yet another language entirely different from the journal entries.

As he read thru them Jeffery realized that they were more journal like then technical entries. They were for a very short and specific time frame. Whomever had inputed them was also quite likely the same person who set up the console initially. According to the paperwork, although this unit was the first device in the series, it was actually the fifth one the man had set up. It had been quite difficult for him to get flown out to this specific location. He explained how they had a variety of ideal locations that they could set up the devices, but they were never sure which one they could get to, so they were setting them up in reverse.

Jeffery smiled, noting that they had four more locations after this one before they would get to the main device. This information was not in the documentation or journals that the government had. So they had an edge on them. It also mentioned that it was pertinent that the devices be activated in order. More so for the host then the device. Jeffery wondered what this meant, but didn't think too much of it. Japanese puzzle boxes had to be done in a specific order or they couldn't be opened. He presumed that this was the same case.

By the time he had finished reading the entries he had come to the conclusion that the author must have been Dr. Fredrickson's assistant. The way he spoke, although similar to the doctors, was also distinctly different. A thought suddenly occurred to Jeffery. Why couldn't Dr. Fredrickson's son have triggered the device back then? Dr. Fredrickson specialized in genetics, so wouldn't he have modified his son? Why did it have to be a descendant? How could he have known for certain that his lineage would have continued? What made Denis any different from any other descendent?

The more Jeffery thought about this, the more his head hurt. He had to figure out what the assistants last name was. So far in all of the journal entries that he had read, Dr. Fredrickson had only referred to him as Charles. Somewhere, somehow, someone had to have written down his full name. He needed to figure it out and quickly.

Conrad, Denis and Jeffery gathered themselves into a large SUV. The Major General was already inside. Despite being a large eight seater SUV, Denis was forced to sit in the back on his own. No one else would accompany them. Conrad drove, the Major General was in the passenger front seat and Jeffery sat in the middle section. This time, Jeffery was less excited then he had been when they flew in the plane. He had come from a wealthy family and they had owned a vehicle of their own. Although, they seldom rode in it, due to extremely high fuel prices, he did spend many a day, in the back seat of the car day dreaming.

"Brings back memories, doesn't it Denis?" Jeffery asked as they drove off in a westwardly direction. They were heading towards Sector 1, formerly known as Colorado.

"Sure does. I did how many girls in the backseat of your parental units car?" Denis said proudly and Conrad laughed as Jeffery's face shrivelled up.

"You did what?" Jeffery proclaimed loudly. "Why did I never know about this?"

"Because that one time, you managed to make out with a girl in the car, you were so proud of yourself. I didn't have the heart to break yours." Denis said chuckling.

Jeffery glared at Conrad. "Did you know about this?"

"Would you believe me if I said no?" Conrad answered, trying hard to stifle his laughter.

Jeffery slumped back in his seat, his arms

crossed over his chest sulking like a small child who just had their favourite toy taken away. The Major General gave Conrad a look and he immediately ceased laughing. Jeffery took no notice in his change of behaviour, nor did Denis who was draped across the entire back seat pretend to make love to a woman, moaning loudly while Jeffery pouted.

"Awww, Jeffy poo, don't be sad." Denis said.

"I'm not." Jeffery said, obviously still upset.

Denis leaned over the seat and grabbed Jeffery's hand. "Here touch it, it'll make you feel better." He said as he put Jeffery's hand on his tattoo. Jeffery shrieked like a girl and tried to pull his hand away but Denis held it tight, stroking it along the tattoo. The cockroach quivered with excitement and Jeffery continue to squeal while Conrad fought to maintain his composure and even the Major General snickered at the commotion behind him. Unable to hold it back any longer the Major General abruptly whistled loudly and everyone, Conrad included, covered their ears and winced. Conrad quickly put his hands back on the steering wheel and glared out of the corner of his eye at the Major General. Denis slumped back into his luxury seat and Jeffery angrily hunched over his notes.

They remained this way for the next several

hours. Alternating between the Major General and Conrad driving. Denis slept the majority of the drive while Jeffery continued to translate the journal. When they arrived the Major General held out his hand and Jeffery handed him the translated the journal as well as the originals that he had just translated. Denis took notice of this, curious as to what had increased the Major Generals distrust.

They had driven to a old water station in the heart of Sector 1. It too, like Sector D had long since been abandoned. It had been the very first Sector created after the first wave of toxins. The world had been allocated into various sectors to better serve humanity. Each sector had been designated based on its capability to contribute productively to humanity as a whole. There were many more abandoned sectors then there were operational, but Denis did wonder if the all the devices were placed in sectors that were created in Dr. Fredrickson's time line. It would make the most sense. He also wondered if Jeffery could figure this out on his own and if they could use it to their advantage at some point. Denis didn't like the fact that there was yet another faction already looking for the devices and that they seemed to be as knowledgable as the government. It made him wonder about the governments true motives were and if they really had all the available information.

As soon as Denis stepped out of the car he felt his tattoo pulse. Trembling as if it might any second fly away off of his cheek. He could feel it struggling to contain itself within his skin. Jeffery grabbed his arm and whispered into his ear. Jeffery broke away just as quickly and followed the Major General into the building. As they stepped into the building they entered a small room filled with full body protection suits. Conrad entered last and sealed the door behind them. The four of them donned the suits, checked each other for leaks and then the Major General entered a sequence of key codes into a keypad, unlocking the door that led further inside.

Denis and Jeffery went first. Denis being led by the tattoo and Jeffery keeping an eye out for potential obstacles. Denis was not paying any attention to where they were walking as the tattoo was screaming much louder than his senses could tolerate. The recent release of the chlorine gas in the facility was aggravating his tattoo immensely. Conrad took up the rear, keeping an eye out for anyone that may have survived the high dose of chlorine. When they had sent the first team out to release the gas, they had informed the Major General that the gas wasn't able to fully penetrate the entire building and that there may be pockets of unaffected air. If the other faction was already hiding within they may have found somewhere safe to hide. Otherwise, the chances of anyone being able to follow them now was limited as they had also brought in the remaining suits.

The first team had assured the Major General that from within the facility they would be able to flush the chlorine gas out of the air. They couldn't risk Denis dying when he had to exposed the tattoo to the scanner.

They made their way thru the relatively small plant and into a small lunch room. In the centre was a curved table. Denis made a beeline for it and proceeded to try and find a way to activate the device buried within it. Jeffery examined the room looking for a way to flush the chlorine out. Unable to find anything obvious inside the room Jeffery and Conrad left the room together to hunt down the filtration switch. The Major General watched Denis as he continued to struggle with the table. Denis looked at him and pointed at the table shrugging his shoulders. The Major General stared at him, blatantly ignoring his request.

The sound of air being vacuumed out of the room was heard. Minutes later Jeffery and Conrad came back into the room, their headpieces in their arms. Denis quickly took his off and inhaled deeply. Jeffery looked at the table and asked Denis if he had had any luck but Denis shook his head no. He began to strip the suit off and was pulling his feet out of his boots when he placed a hand on the table to steady himself. He felt a small pin prick on his finger and yanked his hand off the table. Right before their eyes the table transformed into a console similar to the first one they had already visited.

Jeffery stripped out of his protective gear and joined Denis beside the console. He looked at his notes then entered a sequence of commands into the console. Like before a scanner emerged out and Denis placed his cheek against it. It scanned his cheek and the tattoo dissolved into thin air. A new tattoo slowly appeared on his cheek. A series of swirls and numbers. This time, without any prompting from Jeffery, the console opened up a hole for Denis to place his hand. Denis groaned and looked at Jeffery pleadingly.

"Don't look at me. I didn't build this." Jeffery said, raising his hands in the air feigning innocence.

Denis sighed and slid his hand into hole and like the previous time it sucked his arm in and held him firmly in place. This time it pricked his arm multiple times with a tiny sharp needle.

Denis screamed out in pain as the console spit out more papers into Jeffery's eagerly waiting hand. Jeffery slid the pages into his journal with no one the wiser. The console abruptly let go of Denis's arm and he flew backwards, kicking at it as he fell to the ground. There were several puncture marks on his arms, a few of which were oozing blood.

"What the hell did it do to you?" Conrad proclaimed loudly as he examined Denis's arm up close. Denis guarded his arm close to his chest and growled at Conrad. Conrad rolled his eyes before noticing that the Major General had already left the room. "C'mon, lets go before we're left behind." Conrad said pulling Denis to his feet.

As they left the room Denis shot Jeffery a dirty look. "Next time tell it to be a bit more gentle in its distraction. I feel like a bloody pin cushion." Denis growled. Jeffery looked at him flabbergasted.

None of them noticed that as they left the room a door directly behind the console swung open. Inside it, wearing a gas mask and in clear view of where the console had made the handoff to Jeffery, was Chuck.

"Strip." She ordered him.

Denis blinked, looking at the woman in front

of him.   "Excuse me?" he asked uncharacteristically flustered.

The woman was long limbed and toned. She had white blonde hair that reached her buttocks even when pulled back in a high ponytail. Her eyes were an emerald green and her skin smooth and porcelain like. She was incredibly beautiful and looked like she came from one of Jeffery's books. Her beauty was marred only by the stony hard look on her face.

"I said strip." She repeated, with no less authority than the first time. "And do behave, you're not my type." A red flush crept across his cheeks.

"Now." She ordered as she slapped a glove onto her hand. Denis awkwardly stood up from the bed that he had been sitting on. He turned his back to her and stripped down to his skivvies. "Everything off." She said without even glancing at him. Denis tried to protest but she gave him a look that would make any life wither. He humbly removed his skivvies and sat back down on the bed, his hands over his privates.

She stepped in front of him, flashlight in one hand and plastic tongue depressor in the other. She instructed him to open his mouth and she peered into his throat.   She made him look in every direction possible while she examined his eyes and ears. She mapped out the pin pricks on his arms onto a chart, indicating their size and redness. The majority of them had subsided during the drive back, with only a few staying vibrantly red and sensitive to the touch. She had Denis stand up while she inspected his legs closely. Satisfied she stood up to face him.

"Turn around." She instructed and he obliged. "Bend over." She said and he began to squawk, insisting that nothing had gone anywhere near there. "Now, I don't know that. I wasn't there. You could have been compromised." She said firmly as she roughly pushed him over the bed.

Denis yelped, he closed his eyes and winced noiselessly. It was over quickly and by then his hands were clenching the bed so tightly that his knuckles were white. Anything his hands had been trying to hide was now long gone.

She ordered him to sit back down and he silently complied. She disappeared briefly and returned with a rolling tray filled with syringes and several empty capsules. Without any resistance he let her draw his blood and then inject him with a milky white substance. She applied another milky white gel to the puncture marks on his arms and began to jot notes down on her clipboard.

"You may go." She said.

"Uhhh, this is my room." Denis said, "and

you owe me 100 cred for that, umm, service I provided." He finished, his cockiness slowly returning.

She looked up from her clipboard and smiled softly. He raised his eyebrows in disbelief. But before he could say anything else, she set her clipboard on the rolling tray and left the room.

Once dressed Denis left his room and headed towards the mess hall. The doctors visit had to his surprise, worked up an appetite he hadn't felt since before he activated the first device. He had been overwhelmingly nauseous and hadn't been able to bring himself to consume much more than liquids in the last few days. The doctor must have done something right as he not only felt his appetite for food return but his stomach was beginning to settle as well. At the thought of her he felt an appetite for her growing in his loins as well.

He walked into the mess hall to find it empty aside from the cooks. It was well past noon so he had missed the lunch rush and was too early for dinner. He had hoped that there would still be something for him to eat. Something simple. His stomach lurched slightly at the smell of food and he wasn't sure if it was in anticipation or dread. One of the cooks saw him and told him to wait while they disappeared into the back.

When they returned they held a tray that had three bowls and a small plate. One bowl held a clear broth, the other two milky white substance with random 'meat' chunks. The plate held several small biscuits. The cook held it out to him, chirping about doctors orders and Denis begrudgingly took it.

He sat down eyeing the milky broth suspiciously. It bothered him that what he was about to eat highly resembled what the doctor had just injected into him. He broke a biscuit in half finding it surprisingly fluffy. He gave a half cocked smile as he dipped it into the soup.

"Hello handsome." A female voice said and Denis turned to face her, hoping it may be the doctor coming for another round. The woman who was now sitting to his right was almost as pretty as the doctor but was, unfortunately, not her.

"Hello." Denis said as he resumed eating.

She sidled up closer to him, put a hand on his thigh and coyly slid it all the way up. He felt his loins stir slightly. He put his hand on hers, gently lifted her hand off of his leg and placed it onto her own leg.

"Sorry, I'm trying to eat right now. Doctors orders" He said, hiding the smile on his face as he thought to himself that he still had it.

She moaned softly as she leaned in close and

nibbled at his ear. Denis closed his eyes as he felt her put a hand back onto his thigh. This time she didn't stop and clutched his loins tightly. He gasped softly. She continued to peck at his neck, his chin and his cheek. As she clutched his loins again she bit deeply into his cheek. He yelped and shoved her to the ground, clutching his cheek.

"What the hell?" Denis cried out, looking at his hand covered in bright red blood. His blood.

The woman got to her feet, her movements cat like in nature, licking her lips as she wiped his blood from her face. She swallowed dramatically and Denis shuddered. She grinned, her teeth stained pink and he jumped to his feet, grabbing his tray and sending his meal flying.

"A little help please." Denis called out, glancing over his shoulder to see that he was now completely alone in the mess hall aside from bat shit crazy lady. "So, you know that they have this thing called food, right? You can get it right there." Denis said pointing to the food counter.

"Denis must die." She said slowly and meticulously as she stepped closer to him, a knife mysteriously appearing in her hand.

"Oh, you have the wrong person then. My name, is, um, Conrad. That's right. I'm

Conrad." Denis said stumbling. He wasn't afraid of fighting her, but his stomach had begun to act up again and it was taking most of his energy to hold himself upright. His arms had begun to throb intensely and he could see the tray shaking in his hands.

"The traitor must die." She cried out as she jumped at him slashing her knife thru the air. Denis held the tray out in front of his face but her knife cut thru it easily. He managed to grab her wrist and they tumbled over together. He pushed her knife hand to the side, narrowly missing his face. As they hit the ground he groaned and tossed her to the side. He rolled onto his knees and pulled himself onto his feet, an arm clutched tightly around his stomach. The tattoo on his cheek began to throb.

"Why am I a traitor. Can't we talk about this?" Denis said desperately as he scanned the room. She was now between him and the only way out. If he could get out into the hall it was only a few steps from the mess hall to the crews quarters where he would likely find somebody who could help him. Unless of course, they were the ones trying to kill him. Given the high level of security at the base it was likely that this was an inside job. Chances of Chuck's crew infiltrating the base was highly unlikely.

The woman rushed at Denis again and he

tried to dodge her, only to receive a gash along the side of his arm. He yelped as the knife burned his skin. She laughed as he doubled over in pain. "If I play with you long enough, the poison will do the job for me." She said as she grabbed Denis by the hair, lifted his head up and then thrusted her knee into his chest. He fell to the ground moaning in pain.

"I thought Chuck wanted me alive. He should know better." Denis mumbled.

She knelt down beside him and held the knife against his throat. "Who's Chuck?" she asked.

"Your boss you idiot." Denis said and she slapped his face with the knife handle. Blood spurted from his nose and he rolled onto his side, clutching his tattoo which had begun to hum softly.

"I don't know who this Chuck is, but he is not my boss. We don't want you alive. Alive, you're a risk to us all and everything we stand for. Your ancestor killed our leader, who was trying to protect us from the devastation that he would bring us all." She held the knife against his throat and began to press. "Your lineage ends with you. Everything will die with you." She said smugly.

Denis clenched his eyes closed, annoyed at the fact that a stomach bug would lead to his demise. He felt the knife press against his throat and then just as quick it was gone. His eyes briefly fluttered open and he could see halos of light above his head. A blurry image of Conrad and Jeffery hovered above him. They looked like angels passing judgement on his soul. Denis reached a hand out to them as everything began to spin and his world went black.

Chapter 8

"Missed me already did you?" The doctor said as Denis's eyelids began to slide open. He tried to sit up but she gently pushed him back down. He didn't resist. "Easy does it big boy. That was a pretty lethal does of poison that she gave you."

"Stupid biscuits." Denis mumbled and the doctor laughed.

"Smart biscuits." She said as he protested. "The poison was in two parts. Part of it was in the biscuits. But its catalyst was in the soup. Since biscuits are porous, they absorbed the liquid quickly and therefore brought a large dose of poison to your system in a short period of time."

"Stupid biscuits." He muttered and the doctor smiled.

"Agreed."

She went about checking his vitals and he

watched her closely. Gliding like a leaf in the breeze falling onto a pond. Denis was sure that was the poison affecting his mind. Jeffery came in and Denis could hear the two of them talking about his condition. After a few minutes she left Denis alone with Jeffery, who sat down beside him and began to read thru his journal. Jeffery looked up at Denis long enough to inspect the ever fluctuating tattoo on his cheek. Earlier, before he passed out, Denis could have sworn the tattoo was singing to him. Moments later Conrad stopped by to check up on him. Satisfied with Denis's current condition Conrad quickly left.

Jeffery set his book down on his lap then closed it. He got up, inspected the hallway and then closed the door to the med bay.

"I'm beginning to not like it here." Jefferey said quietly.

"You liked it here?" Denis said confused, the drugs still muddling his mind.

Jeffery gave him an annoyed look. "You know what I mean."

"Sure buddy." Denis mumbled.

Jeffery sighed. "I don't trust them. They're up to something."

"Yeah. World domination. Don't you remember what the Major General said."

"It has to be more than that. Why else would

they keep hiding things from us? What could be worse than world domination?" Jeffery asked aloud.

"That psycho bitch from the mess hall?" Denis chortled. Jeffery laughed with him. "You think Chuck would have found someone better to kill me." Denis grumbled.

Jeffery shook his head. "It wasn't Chuck."

Denis's laugh turned into a coughing fit. Jeffery poured him a glass of water and helped him to drink it. "Of course it was Chuck, Conrad can't kill me. Yet." Denis said sadly.

"It couldn't have been Chuck, look." Jeffery pulled a piece of paper from his journal. He helped Denis to a seated position so he could read the note.

"English, how original." Denis said with a laugh.

"Chuck isn't exactly a linguist." Jeffery said seriously. "Nor does he have good penmanship."

"No shit. How the heck did you manage to understand his chicken scratches?"

"Its a warning." Jeffery said.

"Exactly. Warning us that he's going to kill me."

"Not exactly. Warning us that there are other factions out there. Key word 'factions'. As in plural. Many of them want your head." Jeffery said.

"Why? What did I do now?"

"Apparently Dr. Fredrickson defected from his original group of mad scientists and they were always a bit pissed off at him for that. His defection got the majority of them killed." Jeffery stated matter of factly.

"How does Chuck know this sorta shit and why do you believe him so easily." Denis asked as he drank more water. Most of it dribbling down his chin as his mouth was still numb from the poison.

"I think Chuck must have journal entries that we don't have. Some of what he's said coincides with what I've already translated. He knows things that only I should know. From the printouts."

Denis grabbed the sheet from Jeffery and looked it over. "How did you get all of that information from one little note?" he demanded.

"I...uh..." Jeffery stammered as Denis eyed him suspiciously.

Before Jeffery had a chance to answer the med bay door opened and the doctor returned. She instructed Denis to lie back down. She gave Jeffery a knowing look and asked him to leave so Denis could rest. That he needed to sleep off the poison. The more energy he exerted the longer it would take to wear off. She examined the wound on his cheek then the tattoo before shooting Jeffery another look. He quickly scampered off. Denis mumbled out to him as he left, trying to force coherent words to come out. The doctor gently stroked his face and kissed his injured cheek as he drifted off into slumberland.

Denis was back in his room dressed only in pants as he sat on his bed tying his sneakers. Conrad let himself into his room and kicked the bed frame. Denis ignored him as he finished tying his laces. He stood up and pulled a fresh shirt out of the locker. The bruises on his torso gleamed brightly in the florescent lighting. Conrad stood there watching him.

"Are you just going to stand there like a pervert watching me get dressed?" Denis asked, the annoyance in his voice obvious. He had spent the last 48 hours in the med bay recovering. Jeffery hadn't come by since his initial visit despite the numerous times Denis had asked him too. Then when Denis had seen him in the mess hall earlier that morning Jeffery had jumped out of his seat and scurried out. It annoyed him to no end that Jeffery was obviously avoiding him. The little twerp was holding out on him and putting their efforts with the government at risk.

"Bit pissy aren't we big boy." Conrad snarked.

"Well, lets see, the tattoo on my face feels more alive and painful then the bloody cockroach did. It even likes to sing me to sleep sometimes. The device thinks I'm a pincushion and you guys let a psycho bitch into the base who not only poisoned me but thought I was a flippin' entrée. So you tell me." Denis countered angrily. He just wanted to find Jeffery, corner him for a moment and potentially beat the info out of him. He didn't have the time nor the desire to deal with Conrad and his pettiness at the moment. He picked his hoodie up off of the bed and made his way to leave the room. Conrad held an arm out blocking his way.

/ "Now is not the time to pick a fight with me, Conrad." Denis said thru clenched teeth.

"I'm sorry should I let you go whine to your darling Jeffery about big bad evil Conrad?" Conrad said sarcastically.

Denis grinned like the Cheshire Cat. "Sounds good to me." He said as he pushed himself past Conrad.

Conrad put a hand on his chest and pushed him back onto the bed. Denis immediately jumped to his feet, his fists ready to punch. Conrad held his hands up in truce.

"Except Jeffery may be the last person you want to talk to right now." Conrad said, producing a folded up piece of paper between his fingers. He tossed it at Denis.

Denis eyed him carefully but opened the paper up. He read it twice then looked at Conrad with disbelief. "Where did you find this?" he demanded.

"Under Jeffery's pillow." Conrad said smugly.

"Bullshit."

"Along with the notes that the device has been 'secretly' spitting out to him." Conrad said as Denis stared at him with surprise. "Did you really think that we hadn't noticed?"

Denis went to reply but kept his mouth shut instead. He glared angrily at Conrad who laughed as he left the room. "Give my regards to Jeffy poo." Conrad said. Denis, his fists curled up tightly, punched the wall of his room before storming off to find Jeffery.

Conrad, Jeffery, Denis and a small detailed unit, minus the Major General, walked into the abandoned building. Like the previous two locations, this sector was also abandoned. It was, however, located directly beside another sector that was thriving. A flood had taken this small sector out shortly after it had been built and thusly been rebuilt nearby to make relocation of those who had survived significantly easier. The building they were entering was actually right on the border of the old sector and the new.

The tension between Denis and Jeffery was quite apparent. They walked on either side of Conrad, Jeffery fidgeting with his journal and Denis with a sour look on his face. They easily made their way to the device with no sign of Chuck or any other opposing faction. By now Conrad was convinced that Chuck and his faction were unlikely to make their real move until they got to the final device. According to the researchers there were either three or four more devices like until they reached their main objective. So they were likely to remain uninterrupted until then. At least from Chuck. The other factions were a different story. Security had been tightened but attacks occurred almost hourly wherever Denis was. Despite his anger at Jeffery and the lack of proof, Denis knew there was much more to the puzzle then anyone was willing to tell him. Even when Conrad had given Denis his absolute assurance that he had thoroughly investigated all the personnel, Denis had simply told him to just ask Jeffery when the next attack would be. Conrad had eyed the two of them carefully while silently chuckling to himself.

They found the device admits a pile of rubble. Denis let it scan his face. When the hole in the console appeared Denis stared Jeffery hard in the eyes. "No bullshit this time." And stuck his hand in the hole. Although it did grab his hand it only gently pulled him down into the hole and pricked his arm a few times. With his other hand Denis reached under the console and grabbed the papers the console was printing before Jeffery could take them.

As the console let go of his hand a butterfly appeared on his face replacing the swirls and numbers. He stood up, the papers in his hands and shook them in Jeffery's face. "See how easy that was? No need for games and other bullshit." Denis threw the papers in Jeffery's face who stood frozen with shock and surprise. He stormed past Jeffery and Conrad, exiting the room.

As he left, the room began to shake violently. They all fell to the ground as the room continued to shake intensely. Bits of the ceiling and debris raining down on them. Jeffery hid under the console frantically gathering his papers. Denis fell back into the room, knocking over a member of the unit. A loud explosion could be heard from outside the room. Far enough away to be safe but close enough that the noise caused them to cover their ears with their hands and wince.

After a few minutes the shaking abruptly stopped. Denis coughed, the air now filled with thick dust, as he got to his feet and offered a hand to the solider he had knocked down up. Conrad anxiously looked around the room, half expecting the shaking to resume. Jeffery, after gathering the notes, cautiously got to his feet and asked what had happened. Denis barked at him and Jeffery cowered. Conrad instructed them to follow him putting Jeffery and Denis directly behind him with the rest of his detail taking up the rear.

They made their way through the building, the air riddled with dust, dirt, and debris making it difficult to see clearly. Jeffery emerged from the building first coughing loudly. When his coughs finally subsided he cocked his head from side to side.

"Where's the car?" Jeffery asked.

The others looked in the direction where they had left the car. It was nowhere to be seen. Conrad stepped towards where the car should have been with Denis close behind. Conrad hollered out as he felt his feet give out from beneath him and began sliding down a steep slope that had appeared out of nowhere. Denis was barely able to grab his hand in time and pulled him back. They landed on their butts, sitting at the edge of the incline staring off into the dust cloud that hovered above their heads.

A breeze appeared and blew the dust cloud

away. Denis peered over the edge of the incline to see that it went down for what appeared to be miles with no end in sight. Jeffery gasped and they all looked up at the sight before them. Or the lack thereof. As the dust had settled they saw that the neighbouring sector was gone. A large crater like canyon was all that remained of it.

"Denis, wake up." Jeffery called out softly. Denis rolled over, trying to ignore him. He felt Jeffery shake him by the shoulders and he groaned. He pulled the blanket up over his head and pushed Jeffery's hand away. "C'mon Denis, please." Jeffery pleaded. Denis felt a hand hover near his head and instinctively he snatched Jeffery's arm with one hand while the other grabbed his throat. He heard Jeffery squeak and he released the pressure on the throat slightly.

"Jeffery?" Denis asked groggily.

Jeffery squeaked again and Denis pushed him away roughly. He heard Jeffery fall to the floor.

"What the hell do you want?" Denis demanded.

"We need to get out of here." Jeffery said timidly.

"You need to get out of my sight. Now." Denis said as he rolled over away from Jeffery.

"Leave me alone."

Jeffery yanked the blanket off of him. Denis roared as he sat back up and tried to snatch the blanket back.

"Please, Denis, its not safe for us here anymore." Jeffery pleaded.

"The only one in danger right now is you." Denis growled.

"They didn't care that an entire sector was wiped out Denis. The Major General didn't even bat an eye when Conrad told him what had happened." Jeffery said. Denis sat up with a huff, rubbing the sleep out of his eyes.

"What did you expect? Casualties of war."

"We're not at war Denis."

"Yes Jeffery, we are. Only no one realizes it anymore. We're at war with ourselves." Denis stated.

Jeffery sighed and sat down beside Denis. "How long before they kill the two of us?" Jeffery asked.

Denis turned to face, his anger replaced with contempt. "You long before me." He replied.

Jeffery shuddered and stood up. "Denis." He said softly.

"Go, traitor." Denis said quietly, the anger quickly rising back.

The sound of footsteps marching down the hall could be heard approaching the room.

"Denis, no." Jeffery pleaded, his eyes tearing over.

"Traitor." Denis shouted as the soldiers rushed into his room and took Jeffery by the arms. They ushered Jeffery out into the hallway where Denis heard a female voice order the troops to let the prisoner go. That she would take him from here. The troops protested but she quickly cut them off. Denis heard them march off down the hallway followed by the clacking of her heeled shoes and the patter of Jeffery's soft soled shoes following her. Denis flopped back onto the bed, his eyes welling up with tears. He growled angrily at himself before punching the now battered wall. Closing his eyes he cursed Jeffry then rolled onto his side, curling up into a ball. He clutched his pillow tightly with his fingers curling at the edges. He could feel something under his pillow. Sitting up Denis reached under the pillow and pulled out a small journal. Unlike the others, which were a collection of separate pages gathered into one, this one was fully intact. It was also significantly smaller than the others being less than half the size and fit easily in the palm of his hand.

Denis opened it up and quickly scanned it. It was written in yet another language, different than the rest of the documents they had gathered. If he was correct, it was written in German. A language long since banned after the third world war. He recalled when they were in high school Jeffery had gotten excited when he had found a book on how to learn German. The history books that he had read stated that anyone caught speaking or reading German after WWIII were to be immediately executed on the spot. So of course they had to learn it. Denis had eagerly learned with Jeffery so the two of them could talk in secret around Conrad. Anything to annoy their friend.

His eyes welled up again, this time with frustration. As he flipped through the book a single page fell out onto his lap. He opened it to find a single sentence. *'Be safe my friend. ~ Jeffery'*

Chapter 9

Jeffery looked at the door in front of him then the note in his hand. He saw that he was alone in the dark alley. He took a deep breath before knocking on the door. A small slot in the door slid open and an eyeball stared him down. He heard a grunt then the slot abruptly closed. Silence followed as Jeffery awkwardly stood at the door, waiting. After several minutes he crumpled the note, shoving it into his pocket as he turned to leave. The sound of latches sliding and the creaking of the door slowly opening stopped him in his tracks. He turned back to see Chuck.

"Welcome, we've been waiting for you." Chuck said, a smile on his face.

The doctor walked into Denis's room whipping the blanket off of him with one hand while the other pushed a rolling cart inside. She smiled as she realized he was naked and turned away as he curled himself up into a ball.

"Christ lady, a little warning." Denis grumbled.

"If you weren't sulking like a baby in your room I wouldn't need to go to such extremes, now would I?" she retorted haughtily.

Denis sat up and grabbed the blanket, shoving it in front of him as he walked over to his locker to grab clothes.

"Sit down. You don't need those, yet."

Denis looked at her, his heart sinking. She laughed at the expression on his face as he sat back down on the bed, dejected. She went to his locker, pulled out his skivvies and threw a pair at his head. "You can put these on. For now." She said playfully.

She took his temperature and checked his vitals. Denis watched with great interest as she gracefully moved about. As she was listening to his heart beat Denis took her free hand in his. They locked eyes briefly before he put her hand on his loins and smugly smiled. "This still good?" Denis asked.

She squeezed hard and he yelped, falling over, his hands between his thighs, curling up into a ball again.

"Yup, they seem to be functioning well." She

said as she snapped her glove. "You weren't due for this examination for awhile yet, but I should check just to be safe."

She yanked his skivvies down, spreading his legs apart, laughing as he whimpered. She leaned over him, her hand hovering near his buttocks and her mouth near his ear.

She whispered softly. "I can behave if you can."

He nodded eagerly as she stood up, taking her gloves off. He pulled his skivvies up and mumbled an apology to her. She went about preparing a shot. He diligently sat up straight as she administered the shot. As she untied the rubber band around his arm she leaned in close.

"If you're going to ignore your mating tattoo, the least you can do is learn how to properly flirt with a woman." She whispered into his ear then kissed him softly on the cheek.

As she moved away Denis grabbed her by the arm and pulled her close. They gazed deeply into each others eyes. His lips brushed hers softly and her eyes closed. As his tongue grazed her lips she abruptly broke away from him and began to fuss with her tray. His arm fell limply to his lap and he blinked dumbly as she pushed the cart of the room.

The elevator shaft trembled and shook. Conrad,

Denis and two other unit members had squeezed into the tiny elevator that would take them several feet down into the ground.

"Are you sure this is where the next device is?" Denis asked Conrad. "Given what happened last time, I'm not exactly comfortable going down into a mine."

Conrad nodded in agreement. "The researchers are fairly certain, yes."

Denis gave him a look. "Fairly certain? So not 100% certain?"

Conrad squeezed his arm, pulled him in close and hissed into his ear. "We both know that traitor was smarter than my entire team combined, but even he was never completely certain. Yet you trusted him. So trust me now."

Denis roared with laughter. "Trust the man that wants to kill me?"

"Want to and going to, are two very different things." Conrad said through clenched teeth.

Denis looked at him sadly, wondering how and when everything had fallen apart. First he had lost their parental units, then Conrad and now he had lost Jeffery. Denis wondered if how Conrad looked at him was the same way Denis looked when he thought of Jeffery. He had hoped not. No one should look at anyone with that much contempt and hatred.

"I'm sorry." Denis said and Conrad looked at

him skeptically. Denis gave a weak smile of encouragement and Conrad relaxed slightly.

They rode the rest of the long ride down into the bowels of the mine shaft in silence.

They hit the bottom with a lurch. Denis quickly slid the metal gate open and burst out of the elevator. He inhaled deeply then immediately gagged. The air was thick and stale. He wondered how long they could safely remain down there. Conrad looked around the narrow shaft and indicated for his men to flank either side of Denis. Denis watched them as they went onto full alert.

"What is it?" Denis asked Conrad.

"Someone else is already here." Conrad replied, pushing Denis behind him.

"How can you tell?" Denis asked.

"Aside from the obvious?" Conrad said smugly, pointing to the ground where there were several footprints scattered about.

"Its a mine shaft with zero air circulation. Those could be from decades ago. They stopped mining well over a century ago in most sectors." Denis said, shaking his head.

Conrad pulled him down closer to the ground. "Look at that one, where I just stepped and looked at the one beside it. You can see the difference."

Denis studied it closely and after a few moments he admitted that he could see a slight difference between the two. Conrads print was visible 'fresher' and the dirt was brighter colour. The dirt in the other foot prints had faded subtly with time. It was incredibly subtle and Denis doubted that anyone other than Conrad would have noticed a detail like that.

"Which way is the device?" Conrad asked.

Denis stood up and slowly rotated himself in a complete circle. With his eyes still closed he pointed to his left.

Conrad stood alert and barked orders to his men. "Exactly where the new footprints are headed. Everyone be on guard. There are potentially two factions out there and one of them is out to kill. We need to protect Denis at all costs."

Conrad took the lead, with Denis directly behind him and the two soldiers in the rear. His old military training kicked in and Denis, despite being weaponless, followed Conrad in a similar fashion. His back was close to the wall, his eyes focused everywhere and his movements quiet and precise. As they reached an intersection Denis would gently tap Conrad on the shoulder in the direction that they wanted to go. They moved together as a group, silent and efficient. At one point Conrad handed Denis a small gun. As they neared the device Denis grabbed Conrad by the collar and indicated an open doorway that lay just in front of them huddled amongst the rocks.

Conrad indicated for his men to flank the doorway and go in first. As they went in, Conrad and Denis flanked the doorway. They heard the sound of scuffling of feet and Conrad burst into the room with Denis hot on his heels. They were immediately surrounded by Chuck and his men.

"Hello gentlemen." Chuck said. "I believe you have something that I want."

"Over my dead body." Conrad said through gritted teeth.

"Oh that can be easily arranged." Chuck said, "But your friend here, for reasons unknown to me, would rather that you live. For now."

Conrad and Denis looked at each other confused. From behind Chuck, Jeffery stepped out of the shadows.

"Traitor." Conrad roared and he rushed towards Jeffery, aiming his gun at him. One of Chuck's men intervened, knocking Conrad to the ground and sending his weapon flying. He jumped back up to his feet and was immediately got knocked back down by two men.

"Jeffery?" Denis said in disbelief. "Why are you with them?"

Jeffery looked at the ground uncomfortably.

"Have they hurt you? Did they force you to help them?" Denis asked, his voice wavering yet hopeful.

Chuck walked over to Jeffery and put an arm around his shoulders. "Jeffery came to us of his own accord. And you should too." Chuck said, grinning like the cat that ate the canary.

Denis looked between Conrad, Chuck and Jeffery. He looked at Conrad apologetically and glared at Chuck. He walked towards Chuck, who continued to grin. Denis caught Jeffery and held his gaze as he walked towards Chuck. When he stopped directly in front of Chuck he turned to face Conrad and apologized. Chuck roared with laughter as Denis turned to face him and proceeded to punch Chuck square in the gut. His laughter cut off abruptly as he doubled over in pain. Denis grabbed Chuck and easily wrestled the gun out of his hands and tossed it over to Conrad.

Conrad shot the two men that stood over him then got back onto his feet. Chuck pulled himself upright and grabbed Denis, pushing him backwards until they hit the wall behind Denis. Jeffery slipped away into the shadows as the two groups fought. Conrad and his men quickly took out most of Chucks crew while Chuck clawed at Denis like a rabid animal.

Screaming at him how they were supposed to work together and how Denis was betraying the mission. Chuck spewed out profanities about Denis and his his parental units. About the nightmares Denis had as a child. Asking if he still had them now. How he hadn't wasted his whole life looking after a lowlife like Denis just to have him screw it all up now. Chuck kept going on and on in an angry frenzied rant.

Conrad's men pulled Chuck off of Denis who was in shock. Chuck looked around the room and saw that he now at a disadvantage. He abruptly took off. Conrad sent his men after Chuck. Conrad looked at Denis and saw how shook up he was.

Denis crumpled down to the ground. Conrad knelt down beside him, shaking his shoulder gently. "C'mon you big lug, don't let some petty words throw you off."

Denis looked up at him, his eyes vacant and hollow. "Did you hear what he said?"

Conrad shook his head and avoided Denis's gaze, lying thru his teeth. "I was too busy trying to save your ass to pay attention."

"He knew things. Things about me. About us." Denis muttered.

"Of course he does. He wants to shake you up. They probably investigated you just as much as we did." Conrad said trying to pull

Denis to his feet.

"He knew about them." Denis said, his eyes wide.

"Who?" Conrad asked carefully.

"My parents."

"Parental unit information isn't a secret dumbass." Conrad said shaking his head.

Denis clutched at Conrads jacket and pulled him closed. "Not my parental units, my parents."

Conrad paused hesitantly and looked around the room. They were still alone. "You mean those stories you used to tell, that wasn't some BS you just made up to impress us?"

Denis nodded. Conrad stood up and scratched his head. His eyes darted back and forth as he pondered what Denis said. He knelt back down to Denis.

"I swear, I've not told anyone." Conrad said quickly. He was visible flustered and growing more anxious by the moment. "Say you believe me." He said urgently.

Denis nodded his head. "I never thought you believed me anyways. Jeffery always felt I was telling stories to try and top the ones he found."

"Jeffery must have told him." Conrad said suddenly.

Denis shook his head. "Chuck knew things I've never told either of you. Things I've told no one."

They sat staring at each other in silence. Denis's life was intertwined with lies upon lies. Truths buried so far deep down that they could shake the government apart in a heartbeat. Conrad grabbed his face and squeezed it hard, turning it to the side.

"Shit." Conrad said, "Dammit it all to hell."

"Whubb?" Denis asked, sounding like a duck with his mouth squeezed into fish lips.

Conrad let go of his face. "Your tattoo, it got damaged in the scuffle."

Denis touched his cheek and shrugged his shoulders. The throbbing of pain felt no different to him than the throbbing of the tattoo. Conrad stood up and pulled Denis to his feet.

"We don't have time to waste pondering how Chuck knows what he does. Lets get this over and done with so we can get back to the base. Figure out our next steps more carefully." Conrad said.

Denis nodded in agreement and walked over to the console. He pulled out a set of translated instructions from the researchers. They contained the sequence of commands he was to input into the console. He quickly scanned them and realized that they were incorrect in a few spots. From memory, he inputted what he had seen Jeffery previously do. The scanner popped up and he put his face on it. The scanner chirped as it scanned, taking much longer than normal to scan the tattoo. It chirped repeatedly and Conrad, keeping an eye on the door, asked Denis what was taking so long. Denis shrugged his shoulders, careful to hold his head still. Conrad glanced down the hall and then satisfied, went over to Denis.

"What do you see?" Denis asked.

"Hmm, part of the tattoo has disappeared, but the area where your cheek is injured it's still lingering." Conrad mumbled.

Denis went to pull his face away but Conrad stopped him. "Don't. I think its trying to work past the injuries to identify the tattoo. If you pull away now it may think you're an imposter." Conrad said as his voice trailed off softly at the implication of his words. He patted Denis on the shoulder and quickly took post back at the doorway. "Don't move and good luck."

Denis muttered obscenities under his breath, but held his face still. After what seemed like an eternity, the scanner finally stopped chirping and disappeared back into the console.

Conrad looked back at him. "Is it done?" he asked. Denis turned his cheek so Conrad could see it. He gave Denis a thumbs up.

Denis input more commands into the console and the hole for his hand appeared. He put his hand into the hole and as expected it grabbed him. He felt the pricks of needles and a slight tingling on his cheek. Then the console made an abrupt honk, followed by a squealing of gears. It abruptly ejected his hand. He touched his cheek but felt nothing new.

"Conrad?" Denis asked, turning his cheek to him. Conrad looked at his cheek, shook his head and then back into the hall.

"Try it again." Conrad suggested.

Denis put his hand back in and it again rejected him. Conrad cursed aloud. He waved Denis over to him and instructed him to go thru his pack.

"What exactly am I looking for?" Denis asked.

"My medipack."

Denis dug thru the pack until he came across a medium sized white cloth box. He opened it and held it out towards Conrad. Conrad rustled through it and pulled out a six inch long, two inch wide device that looked like it had a glow stick inserted in the underside of it. Conrad handed it over to Denis. Bewildered, Denis held it in his hand, looking it over.

"Is this what I think it is?" Denis asked, appalled.

Conrad shook his head. "The tattoo won't appear on your face probably because its damaged. This will hopefully fix it."

"Are you insane?" Denis asked.

"It works." Conrad insisted.

"On dead bodies you idiot. You want to use this on me?" Denis cried out.

Conrad took the device back. "I can and I will." He insisted.

"Over my dead body."

"If that's what it takes."

Denis took a step backwards away from Conrad. Conrad grabbed his arm and Denis punched him in the face. "C'mon. Lets see who's stronger."

"Dammit Denis, we can't afford to waste time. It'll take days to get back to base, even longer for your face to heal and then what? We can't sit here and wait. We need to get out of here as quickly as possible."

Denis, still ready to pounce, eased up. He ran his hands through his hair. "Dammit. I hate it when you're right."

"Now come here and let me fix you." Conrad said.

Hesitantly, Denis approached Conrad. Conrad twisted the device and it lit up. He looked at both sides of it, trying to determine which was the end to aim at Denis's face.

"Have you ever used it before?" Denis asked.

Conrad smiled, "Sure." He said, lying through his teeth.

Denis closed his eyes as Conrad brought it closer to his cheek.   The last thing he remembered was the intense pain of his skin ripping away from his face.

Chapter 10

His face, despite the intense heat burning deep within, felt cool at the moment. Little dribbles followed by the trickling of water fluttered on his face. A soft voice whispered gently and brushed thru his hair softly. Denis moaned in his sleep, fighting through the fog that held him back. He was pinned up against a wall and Jeffery was standing before him, instructing the fog to hold him down. From behind Chuck appeared and handed a long bladed knife to Jeffery. With a sinister smile on his lip Jeffery took the knife and thrusted it deep into Denis's stomach.

Denis bolted upright, a scream escaping from his lips. He felt hands on his shoulder gently push him back down. A soft, soothing voice was telling him that everything was alright and that he was only dreaming. He continued to babble on about Jeffery and the knife as the voice kept talking in a soothing tone until Denis finally subsided and passed out from exhaustion.

Hours later, when Denis woke up, he found himself back at the base and in the med bay. To his left was a basin full of water and a cloth sitting on the edge. He was on the far side of the bed and an indentation beside him indicated that someone had just recently been sitting down beside him. He tried to pull himself up to a seated position but struggled greatly. His head throbbed, as did his cheek.

"Ah, you're finally awake." The doctor said as she came into view. She held a tray that was filled with food. "Guess I'll have to share this with you today, won't I?" she said cheerfully. She set the tray down over his lap and helped him to sit up. She put a couple of pillows behind his back to better prop him up. She handed him two cups. One held pills and the other held water. Denis diligently took them.

"This should help with the concussion, but I'm afraid I can't help with the rest of the pain that I can only imagine you are in." She sat down beside him and began to uncover the food on his tray.

"What happened?" Denis asked weakly.

"Aside from using a device that is meant to manipulate dead human cells into something aesthetically appealing on a live human, not much." she said sarcastically. "Seriously, what were the two of you thinking?" she said shaking her head as she picked up a spoon and began to feed him a substance that resembled mud flavoured jello.

"Save the world at all costs?" Denis said meekly.

"Try not to move that side of your face." She instructed him as she spoon him fed the jello.

"What happened after, you know, that?" he asked indicating the tattoo.

"Thankfully, your skin stayed on your face, although it certainly tried to remove itself." She said as she continued to feed him.

Instinctively Denis reached for the tattoo but she gently swatted his hand away from it.

"Then what happened?" Denis asked.

"You immediately passed out. Which is probably the only reason you aren't permanently damaged. As soon as you passed out the Lieutenant Colonel dropped the device. You eventually came too and insisted on trying the device again. This time, instead of rejecting you completely the tattoo took hold, surprisingly enough. Your cheek had almost completely healed. When the device spit out your arm the mine began to fall apart. The two of you barely made it out alive."

He paused, his mouth clamped tightly on the spoon. She tugged at it gently and he parted lips slightly, allowing her to pull the spoon out. She went to give him another bite, but he pushed the spoon aside.

"What happened to the two men that went down with us?" Denis asked.

"No one knows. They weren't topside when the two of you got out." She said softly.

Denis closed his eyes briefly and sighed. "Is this even worth it? Why do people have to keep dying for me?" Denis said, his voice choked with grief.

She gently brushed his face with her hand. "You are a good man, with good intentions. Aren't you Denis?"

He put his hand over hers and held it firmly against his face and sighed contentedly. "I often wonder if I still am. Or if its too late for me to right the wrongs in my life."

"It is never to late to fix things. As long as your intentions are pure, unlike those leading you around here." She said softly.

His eyes popped open and he stared at her with surprise. Her face flushed bright red and she pulled her hand off his cheek. She set the spoon down on his tray and got up. "You appear to be well enough to finish feeding yourself. I'll be back later to check your vitals."

She said rushing out of the room. Denis just stared at her in disbelief.

Jeffery looked up from his notes as Chuck entered the room. He had been squirrelling himself away over his papers the last few days. Chuck dropped a small pile of papers onto the table in front of Jeffery.

"The others are done with these, they can't make heads or tails of them. They're hoping that you might be able to." Chuck said.

Jeffery looked them over quickly and nodded. He dug through his notes and produced two sketches. The first was from an old journal entry. The other was identical, but hand drawn by Jeffery himself and covered with several notations. He handed them over to Chuck.

"What do you think it is?" Chuck asked.

"A spaceship." Jeffery said.

"A spaceship." Chuck said skeptically.

"An alien spaceship." Jeffery said with more vigour.

"An alien spaceship." Chuck said with disbelief.

"Mmm hmm." Jeffery said nodding.

"You realize how crazy that sounds, right?" Chuck said to him, patting Jeffery on the shoulder and shaking his head.

"Any crazier than the notion, that in a time of

self indulgent technology two scientists, on their own, managed to build, in the ground somewhere, a fulling contained infrastructure without any help or anyone noticing?" Jeffery retorted.

Chuck sighed. "Okay. Point taken. But what makes you think that the infrastructure is that large in the first place. No one has found measurements of any kind. It could be the size of this room for all we know or the size of the desk you're sitting at or even a small box."

"You have to take into consideration that when this device was created. Dr. Fredrickson would have wanted something that he could easily hide. Something already underground would be beneficial. Back in the twentieth century humans were obsessed with secrets. As a result there are bases built upon bases built underground. It would have been easy for him to find one, access it and utilize it. None of the history books from that time say where Dr. Fredrickson was actually located. There are no records of his home or his research labs. Nothing." Jeffery said.

"Okay, that potentially proves that whatever we're looking for is buried. Makes sense. Feels like we're after a buried treasure anyway. What else?" Chuck asked.

"Notice the notations along the edges?"

Jeffery asked, pointing to short little lines that ran sporadically along the four edges of the original sketch.

"They're incomplete. Most likely he was keeping count of something as he drew this picture. So what?"

"Look more closely. Where they line up." Jeffery said as he placed a transparent sheet of paper over top of the drawing. He then pulled a straight edge out and drew lines connecting the two most left notches on the top and bottom of the page. Jeffery pointed. The exterior of the ship was a thick solid line. He flipped the paper up. "If you looked closely, you can barely make out a thinner dotted line that intersects the notches. If you connect the dotted line following the notches you have a line that follows the thicker outline of the ship. While it doesn't exactly follow it never goes outside of the exterior line." On the transparent paper Jeffery traced over the lighter line with a dark pencil, going over all of the notches as he did.

"Impossible." Chuck said quietly.

"If the ship is buried, then it would be impossible for them to measure the outside of it. So they added an inside line to the sketch, representing the area they could see and measure." Jeffery said his voice growing more excited by the moment.

"But how big is it? Do they indicate the distance between the notches?" Chuck asked.

"Sort of?" Jeffery said, his face scrunching up and his glasses almost falling off his nose. He pulled out a piece of glass and held it above the sketch. He peered thru it until he found what he was looking for. "Take a look at that."

Chuck leaned forward and peered thru the glass. His jaw dropped as he moved the glass closer then further away. To the naked eye, without the glass, it looked like nothing more that a blob of ink. But thru the glass it was magnified into an incredibly tiny, yet detailed sketch of a human being.

"Any idea how tall the doctor or his assistant was?" Jeffery said coyly.

"He's not physically capable of travel yet." The doctor insisted.

"You do not have the authority to decide that Private." The Major General said sternly.

The doctor crossed her arms over her chest, "With all due respect, Sir, as his physician, I have the authority to inform you whether or not he is physically capable for duty. Not you nor anyone else. I am the head physician here and this is my med bay. You can not and will not take him until he has completely healed. You risk further injuries if you move him now." She said, her voice firm with authority.

"That's a risk I'm willing to take." The Major General barked at her. "Gentlemen?" He pushed the doctor aside as several soldiers rushed into the med bay and gathered a still sleeping Denis out of his bed. Denis began to wake up and instinctively tried to resist. Despite his weakened state, he managed to take out two of the soldiers and was waving a crutch wildly at the remaining soldiers.

"Doctor. Sedate him. That's an order." The Major General said.

The doctor turned to face the Major General and slapped the syringe into his hand. "Do it yourself." She said storming off.

The Major General shook his head and handed the syringe to one of his men. The soldiers managed to take the crutch away from Denis and hold him long enough to administer the sedative. As he slipped back into unconsciousness Denis felt himself hoisted onto someone's shoulders.

"Wake up Denis." Conrad said slapping Denis's face. "Apparently this doesn't work unless you're conscious." Denis sputtered out of consciousness cursing loudly as he mumbled. Denis's fist began to flail about. "Easy boy, its me, Conrad." he said annoyed.

Denis looked around, visibly confused. He realized that he was no longer in the med bay but lying on the ground, in Conrad's arms. In front of them was a device and nearby several soldiers, their weapons trained on him.

"Where am I?" Denis asked, still groggy from the sedative.

"At the next device," Conrad started. "We transported you while you were unconscious. But the device won't work unless you're awake."

Denis laughed. "Dumbasses. Can't get rid of me that easily, can ya?" he said chuckling.

Conrad stood Denis up and pushed him towards the scanner. "C'mon big boy. Put your face in the scanner. Lets get this over and done with already so we can go back home and you can get your beauty sleep."

Denis puckered his lips and leaned towards Conrad trying to give him a kiss. He made loud smacking noises and Conrad grumbled, pushing Denis's face towards the scanner. Denis shoved Conrad, insisting that he could do it on his own. Conrad let go of Denis only to watch Denis's legs buckle as he slid down towards the floor. Before Conrad could catch him, Denis grabbed the console and pulled himself back up.

"Shit, what the hell did you give me. Can I

have another round later?" Denis said sarcastically. Conrad sighed impatiently and motioned his hand towards the scanner.

"You're not so much fun anymore, are you? Always have been a wee bit uptight." Denis mumbled, making faces at him. The soldiers close enough to overhear him stifled their laughter through tightly bit lips. Conrad shot them a look but it didn't stop them from trembling, their shoulders shaking with laughter.

"See, at least they have a sense of humour. Right boys?" Denis laughed as he collapsed face first into the scanner. It chirped to life as it scanned the tattoo on his cheek. Like last time it had difficulty reading the tattoo and abruptly stopped scanning. Denis turned to face Conrad and shrugged his shoulders with a dumb shit eating grin plastered on his face.

"Do it again." Conrad ordered. Denis looked at the soldiers mouthing the word 'uptight' before placing his face against the scanner. Again, it wouldn't read the damaged tattoo. Conrad forcibly held Denis's face against the scanner as it attempted to scan. The scanner disappeared into the console. Conrad began to haphazardly punch the activation sequence in but the console went dark. Conrad pounded his fists into the console screaming obscenities at it.

Denis looked at him with a smirk on his face.

"Oh I bet you think that this is hilarious, don't you? Poor uptight Conrad, losing his shit, because you can't do one simple thing." Conrad yelled into his face.

Denis nodded, the grin on his face gigantic as he slid off the console and passed out before he could even hit the ground.

Conrad growled and barked at the soldiers to remove him and get him into a med bay immediately.

Denis tossed and turned in his sleep. He was in a nearby room in the facility that housed the current device. After he had collapsed Conrad had the soldiers set up a temporary med bay for him. He ordered the needed medical supplies, along with the doctor, to be flown in. Denis was alone in the room; the doctor and soldiers were nowhere in sight. He whimpered in his sleep, sweating profusely. A sticky, green paste lay atop his tattoo. An old natural remedy the doctor had whipped up when she realized where they were located. Conrad had left the doctor to her own devices and remained behind in his tent, sulking. They were all on standby until Denis healed and the console would then hopefully turn back on.

Muffled voices could be heard from outside in

the hall. They were anxious, nervous and speaking in hushed whispers. Someone entered the room and hovered over Denis. He carefully tousled Denis's hair before taking a closer look at his face. Jeffery grimaced at the sight of it, worried it may not heal in time before the tattoo would consume him.

Suddenly they heard footsteps approaching the med bay. His companion hissed at him to hurry. He placed a small journal in Denis's hand, slide his hand under the sheet and squeezed his hand gently. He told his friend that he would be back soon. He then ran to the doorway, glanced down the hall and disappeared into the darkness. Moments later the doctor and Conrad walked into the med bay. Denis rustled in his sleep calling out Jeffery's name. Upset and annoyed Conrad stormed out of the med bay. The doctor squeezed Denis's shoulder then followed Conrad down the hall calling after him.

Denis clenched and unclenched his fist as his eyelids began to flutter open. He called out to Jeffery, but saw that he was alone. He felt something hard under the sheet and pulled it out. He looked at it with question. It was yet another journal. He flipped thru the pages and a folded up piece of paper fell out. He picked it up and unfolded it, straining to read it in the low lighting.

Please forgive me, but you need to stay put. Find the entries that are still missing and get them to me. He'll tell you how."

Denis abruptly sat up then immediately groaned, putting a hand to his head. It rocked dangerously inside. His face ached and he felt like he had survived a fight that he shouldn't have. He re-read the note over and over again, tears creeping into the corner of his eyes as a laugh escaped from his lips. Denis knew that Jeffery wouldn't have betrayed him. Conrad had obviously set the two of them up somehow. But who was the man Jeffery thought would help him?

No longer confined to his bed Denis was able to walk about freely and easily. He was still quite weak, the tattoo was eating away at him from the inside out while his cheek still healed. It had become a battle of time to see who would win. His body or the tattoo. Conrad came by multiple times throughout the day. He spoke very little and came only to look at Denis's face before leaving. Upset at how long Denis was taking to heal. The amount of damage the undertakers cosmetic device had done to his face on a molecular level was a contributing factor to the amount of time it was taking such a small superficial scrape to heal. They had been in the facility almost two weeks now. Given the few days it had taken for them to figure out where the device was located and then how to get there, almost three full weeks had now passed by. Denis wasn't sure how long it would take for the tattoo to consume his entire body., but he was certain that he wouldn't survive another week. In all the scenarios that Denis had imagined his own death, sitting in a chair, reading an old scientists journal penned in ancient German while being consumed by a tattoo hadn't exactly made his list. Hell, it hadn't been a scenario he had ever fathomed. Most of his scenarios had involved going down in a blaze of glory.

In the past two weeks various researchers had joined them in anticipation of the next tattoo clue. Denis had the doctor wheel him over each day so he could look over their research. No one paid him any attention because no one realized that he could read both the language the documents were written in and the language they were translating them into. The doctor would drop him off then leave Denis to his own devices. He would then pore over entry after entry and squirrel away as many pages as he could stuff down his pants without anyone taking notice. Then when the doctor had brought him back to his room, he would feign tiredness and lie down to sleep. After she left Denis would copy the entries into the journal Jeffery had left him then hide it. Later the doctor would return him to the researchers after his 'nap' and he would sneak the papers back into the scattered mess they had strewn across the table. When the doctor brought Denis back in the late evening, after yet another nap, he would find a note in their place with instructions from Jeffery on what entries he was requiring. The pages he had left were gone.

From what Denis could gather, Jeffery had been putting together a blueprint of the modifications Dr. Fredrickson had done, in order to implement the device. Jeffery had instructed Denis to hold out as long as humanly possible. There was only one more scanning device after this. The next device would lead them to the ship and at that point there was no turning back. Jeffery was also convinced that the ship would indeed save humanity. He just hadn't yet been able to figure out how exactly. His current theory was that the ship was like a giant mixing bowl and somehow Denis was the only one able to turn it on. That perhaps another toxin would be released into the atmosphere that would change their physiology again. The other important piece of information that Jeffery had shared with Denis was that the other faction already knew where the next device was located. They had in their possession a detailed account of each device including their specific locations, activation sequences and the various built in failsafes. What they didn't have was the location of the ship, nor what each tattoo would be. After they were unable to persuade Denis to join them, it had been decided that their government insider would provide accurate details of the tattoos as they appeared. It was still unclear if the tattoos were relevant to activating the ship or not.

Denis still didn't have any idea who the insider was, nor why they were afraid to reveal themselves to him. Jeffery obviously knew who it was as the first note from Jeffery had shown up after everyone from the base had relocated to their temporary camp. He wondered if it could be Conrad. He even hoped that it was Conrad. But Denis knew that Conrad would never forgive him.

Chapter 11

The doctor wheeled Denis's down the hall towards the device. Much to Conrad's dismay, the doctor had convinced the Major General that she needed to be present. She had insisted that with Denis's weakened state, he would most likely require medical attention the second the next tattoo transfer was complete. If she was there she could attend to his needs while the rest of them focused on the more pertinent matters. So the doctor, Denis, Conrad and the Major General, followed by a small group of soldiers, marched down the hallway towards the device.

She helped to position Denis in front of the console. It immediately lit up. With her help Denis entered the activation sequence and the scanner popped out. This time, the scanner appeared just above where Denis sat in his wheelchair. He laughed weakly, wondering aloud if he was on candid camera. The others looked at him in confusion and he sighed sadly knowing that Jeffery would have gotten the outdated reference. Denis leaned forward into the scanner and it chirped happily. Satisfied, the scanner continued to chirp loudly as his tattoo dissolved into his face and a new one appeared on his other cheek. The console then grew quiet.

"What, no torturing Denis this time? I've got enough holes in my arm?" Denis said mockingly. He stifled a cough before the console chirped back. Several small needles poked into his leg from the underside of the console. "Senin kadar aşağılık bir yaratıkla karişilaşmadım." He cried out as he kicked the console. It chirped again, as if mocking him before going silent.

The doctor pulled Denis back and began to cut his pants open. He had several new welts on his left leg. "Lets get you back to the med bay." She said looking up at the Major General. "Do you have what you need of him?" she asked haughtily. The Major General simply grunted and dismissed them.

As she left, the others followed leaving Conrad and the Major General alone in the room.

"If I may be so bold, sir." Conrad started and the Major General gave him an approving look.

"You seem a bit soft on her. Despite her defiance towards you." The Major General grunted again and Conrad took a step backwards, apologizing for overstepping his boundaries.

The Major General chuckled. "I suppose you're right, Lieutenant Colonel. A father does tend to dote, doesn't he?" he said coyly, watching Conrad's jaw drop in surprise.

Back in the med bay Denis was arguing with the doctor over how to take his already shredded pants off. She insisted that she help him into the bed first before she would remove his pants. He kept getting to his feet, insisting that he was feeling well enough to remove his own pants. She pushed Denis down onto the bed gently. He let himself be pushed but wrapped an arm around her waist and pulled her down with him. She shrieked as she collapsed on top of him.

"See, I told you that I'm feeling better. Stronger, even healthier. Whatever that console injected me with has brought back my vigour." Denis said defiantly. And to further prove his point he pressed his lower extremities upwards into her pelvic area.

"Mr. Roy." She proclaimed loudly, half fighting him, half giving in.

"Denis. My name is Denis." He said, enjoying

her body wriggling against his. He slide one hand down her back and cupped her buttocks. The other hand he slid upwards grabbing the back of her head as he pulled her face closer to his.

"Denis." She said softly, easily caving in. As their lips met he abruptly stopped and pulled his head back.

"Wait. I don't even know your name. What kind of an ass am I?" Denis proclaimed, proceeding to berate himself.

She laughed. "Jennifer." She said and kissed him.

The sound of footsteps racing down the hall woke them both. They were laying naked in each others arms. His pants and shirt were strewn on the floor in front of the bed but hers had fallen out of sight.

"Jennifer." Denis whispered urgently into her ear. "Wake up. Someone's coming."

Her eyes immediately snapped open and she hopped out of the bed taking the sheet with her. She hid behind the curtain partially closing it. Denis cleared his throat, reached his hand past the curtain and took the sheet from her. She crouched down low, sneaking her clothes close. He tossed the sheet haphazardly over his body as Conrad raced into the room.

"Get dressed, come with me." Conrad ordered angrily.

Denis sat up, stretching and feigning a yawn. He let the sheet fall off as he stood up.

"Christ, a little decency please."

Denis heard a soft giggle from behind the curtain. "Yessir." Denis said loudly as he gave a mocking salute to Conrad.

"Cut the bullshit. This is serious."

Denis pulled his shirt on and unable to find new pants, put the ripped ones back on. "Whats got your panties in a bunch Conrad? They run out of your favourite ration in the mess hall?" Denis asked, pretending to be sincere.

"The last device. It triggered another earthquake." Conrad said. Jennifer gasped and Denis coughed to cover. "What was that?" Conrad asked suspiciously.

"What was what? I coughed. Big deal. How bad is was the earthquake?" Denis asked, leading Conrad out of the med bay.

"It was larger than the last one. It created multiple tsunami's across the planet. Half of the sectors have been completely wiped out." Conrad said quietly.

Denis ran a hand thru his hair. "Holy shit. I thought this thing was supposed to save us, not destroy us."

As they left Jennifer got to her feet, put on her

clothes and ran out of the med bay.

Denis sat alone in his room, back at the home base, forcing himself to read thru the journal quickly. His ability to translate was nowhere near as good as Jeffery's and he found himself growing more and more frustrated with each passing page. He was barely halfway thru the new journal that Jeffery's accomplice had left. So far he found it to be nothing more than a personal diary. Most likely it was Dr. Fredrickson's diary. It revolved primarily around the meeting of his soon to be wife and the birth of their child. There was nothing significant to his research, the secret project or even the toxins themselves. Denis was still trying to wrap his head around the idea of Dr. Fredrickson's wife being impregnated and confirmed pregnant before even meeting her. He deduced that the need for an heir superseded basic formalities. As of current, Dr. Fredrickson was revelling in joy that his wife was indeed pregnant and with a girl. Denis set the journal down then rubbed his eyes. They felt heavy with grit, his brain begging him to keep them closed and give them some much needed rest. But he pushed himself on knowing that time was scarce.

It wouldn't take them long to figure out

where the next device was. Then, it would lead them to the ship. It had already been five days since they returned to base and last Denis had heard they had narrowed it down to two possible sectors. He flipped absently thru the pages. The celebration of Dr. Fredrickson's upcoming wedding, his wife's troubles with the pregnancy, his attempts to help ease her discomfort, the birth of his son, their first anniversary and so forth. Blah, blah, blah Denis thought to himself. What useless dribble had Jeffery given him? He threw the journal to the ground and kicked it under his bed. The diary was absolutely useless.

He got up, stretching as he did, and went to wander down towards the mess hall. It had been hours since he last ate. As he left the room he abruptly stopped. Son? He got on his hands and knees and crawled under his bed. He pulled out the diary and flipped back thru it to the first entry that mentioned a daughter. Dr. Fredrickson said that he met his wife in the spring and she was already pregnant with his child. In that same year during early summer they got married. Mid winter she gave birth to a boy. Denis flipped back thru the pages. She was pregnant with a girl, but she gave birth to a boy.

Denis reached further under his bed and loosened a piece of the floor. Under it was a small box containing a variety of random notes that Jeffery had made before he left. Initially Denis had laughed when Jeffery had wanted to hide them in his room. He accused Jeffery of being paranoid. But Jeffery had insisted that they were incredibly important and that he trusted no one expect Denis. When Jeffery had left they had ripped his room to pieces. Tore out the floor and the walls. Denis had scanned them briefly weeks ago and was positive that something in those notes pertained to the birth of Dr. Fredrickson's child.

Sitting back on his bed Denis flipped through Jeffery's notes. They mostly talked about the toxin released. How it was mostly theory and that they hadn't had the opportunity to test it. Then scribbled in one of the sides in big letters and surrounded them with question marks Denis found what he was looking for.

Due to the overwhelming lack of adolescents on earth, the toxin was initially targeted at adults only. That way, should it fail, the children could still survive. The first round of toxins revealed females to be susceptible to developing illness during the first year after the toxin was released. Many died.

Denis flipped back to the journal entry where Dr. Fredrickson referred to his wife becoming pregnant. He shook his head with shame. He couldn't believe that he had missed it. It was right smack dab in front of him. Dr. Fredrickson went on to explain how miraculous it was since since she was the first human to become pregnant since they released the toxins. Back in his notes Jeffery had explained how future rounds of toxins eliminated such fertility problems before they finally released a toxin that would affect the adolescents. In Dr. Fredrickson's journal there were several entries where he was concerned about his wife's ongoing illness during her pregnancy.

Denis spread the papers out onto his lap. He theorized that if women were physically compromised by the toxin and Dr. Fredrickson's wife had become ill during pregnancy, then, since the baby was a girl, chances were that even if his wife survived, the baby would not. The unborn daughters illness would most likely kill the mother. Which is why she kept getting significantly worse as the pregnancy progressed. They probably had the technology to alter DNA back then, but who would want to change the gender of their child that far along? Dr. Fredrickson must have done it without his wife's consent. Denis flipped a few more pages into the diary then laughed. Dr. Fredrickson didn't specify details, but almost immediately after doing a routine procedure on his wife, she and the baby suddenly became healthy. Dr. Fredrickson kept up with several treatments during her pregnancy despite neither of them growing ill again. Shortly after she had a boy. What was the significance of that? There had to be something that he was missing.

Jeffery was transcribing another note for Denis. He wasn't sure how it tied in completely, but Dr. Fredrickson was overly meticulous and nothing he had done was without purpose and intent. While assembling the blueprint of the modifications made to the ship Jeffery had come across Charles, Dr. Fredrickson's assistant, personal journal. The more Jeffery read the more convinced he became that Charles was significantly more than just a regular person. There were no records of his birth, his parental units or of any existence before he started working with Dr. Fredrickson. It was almost as if he had appeared out of thin air one day.

He did discover a lot more about Dr. Fredrickson. He had won numerous Nobel prizes for his work with genetic mutation and manipulation. He had remapped the human DNA genome to reveal a third strand hidden within one of the helix's. This discovery had led him and others to make great advancements in ending several illnesses and diseases. It was also what led to Dr. Fredrickson and his colleagues developing god like personas. There was little mention of Charles wife, although, she too had mysteriously appeared out of thin air. However, Dr. Fredrickson had taken great interest in their first child, particularly during its gestation period. Charles had given Dr. Fredrickson carte blanche to administer whatever modifications he desired so long as the baby would be a girl.

Just prior to the creation of the initial toxin, Dr. Fredrickson had been focusing on the manipulation of genes in such a manner that 'positive' attributes, like strength and intelligence, would be guaranteed time and time again, regardless of how many generations would pass. Thus weeding out inferior genetic defects entirely. Charles daughter had been the first baby in this step of genetic evolution.

Jeffery shuddered. He wasn't sure if Dr. Fredrickson was the heroic genius he originally thought him to be. The more Jeffery learned about him, the more afraid he grew of him. He wouldn't have been surprised if he discovered that Dr. Fredrickson had genetically manipulated his own son without his wife's knowledge.

He stood up and stretched his legs. As he did, he knocked a book off of the table. He bent over to pick it up and laughed. It was one of the fairy tale books that he and Denis had first found clues in. Jeffery sat down and flipped through it, chuckling softly at the number of pop ups that had been stripped out of it. Overcome with curiosity he began to take apart the remaining pop ups, hoping to find some random easter egg. Unfortunately, he found nothing. Dejected he sat down, flipping thru the book aimlessly. He paused for a moment then flipped thru the pages backwards and forwards. One of the pages moved differently than the rest. He flipped again and stopped partway thru the book. He flexed the page back and forth but felt nothing. He flexed the next page. This page definitely felt different than the others.

Carefully Jeffery ripped the page out of the book and examined it from the side. Using his fingernails, he carefully pried the two pages apart that were glued together. As he tore them apart, an old photograph fell out onto his lap. He laughed as he discarded the pages and picked up the photograph. It was of a set of identical twins. Except one was male and one female. They were both in their mid twenties. Their arms were wrapped around a teenaged girl. The teenager had her arms held up high in the air, palms facing outwards. There was no visible barcode on either of her wrists. Jeffery felt his breath catch as his heart leap into his throat. The teenager looked an awful lot like Chuck. He turned the picture over and on the back was inscribed *'Charles and sister Charleen, daughter Charlotte'.*

"So its true. I really do look like them, don't I?" Chuck said laughing. Chuck took the picture out of Jeffery's hands, looked at the back of it and chuckled. "Its much worse than it looks. I can promise you that."

Jeffery stared at him dumbly. Chuck picked up the note that Jeffery had scribed for Denis and nodded with approval. He grabbed a chair and sat down beside Jeffery. He took Jeffery's hand and placed it on his chest. Jeffery looked at him uncomfortably as Chuck squeezed Jeffery's hand on his chest softly. Jeffery pulled his hand away and clutched it to his chest, his eyes wide open. He looked at Chuck bewildered. Chuck sat there, silent and unmoving. Jeffery reached out and pulled down the collar of Chuck's shirt to reveal a complicated series of binding material on his, no her, chest. Jeffery's hand fell into Chuck's lap as he stared at her with shock and awe. His mind was reeling. Chuck took Jeffery's hand and put the picture back in it.

Jeffery looked at the picture again more

closely and then back at Chuck. Instinctively he grabbed her right arm and pushed her sleeve up. She had a barcode, just like he did. He held it up close to his face and Chuck laughed.

"Do you want to scan it?" Chuck asked him.

Jeffery slowly shook his head from side to side before spitting on her arm. She froze as he rubbed on her barcode, tightening his grip on Chuck's arm. It took a great amount of effort but the barcode began to smear. She yanked her arm away, her expression full of remorse.

"Charlotte?" Jeffery asked incredulously, finally putting all of the pieces together.

Tears formed in her eyes and they spilled over more easily than either of them had expected. She slowly nodded her head..

"Oh my god, you really are her, aren't you?" Jeffery sputtered.

Chuck jumped to her feet, shaking her head violently from side to side. "No. I'm not. I'm Chuck. Charlotte died a long time ago."

Jeffery stood up and put his hands on her shoulders. "Is your mother? Your father?" Jeffery sputtered incoherently, unable to articulate the words properly.

Chuck shook her head, wrapping her arms around herself as she stared off into the distance. "Mother died shortly after father did. They weren't able to function without each other. Dr.

Fredrickson had mistakenly made their twin bond too strong in his genetic manipulations."

"How are you even possible? And why aren't there more of you? You are literally a walking fountain of youth." Jeffery began to stammer, tripping over his words.

"They killed Dr. Fredrickson before he could finish and trapped my father in that ship." Chuck said quietly. "Father had always told me that the ship would fix everything for us and everyone. That we would finally be accepted as equals."

"Why are you telling me this now?" Jeffery asked.

"I've been trying so hard to activate the ship. All these centuries. On my own. I'm so alone." Chuck said, starting to cry. "If Denis doesn't activate the ship then humanity is doomed and I'll be alone forever."

Jeffery shook his head. "I'm pretty sure, that despite all of his best efforts, he has at least a dozen illegitimate children out there."

"It doesn't work that way." Chuck said as she grabbed Jeffery's hand and led him out the room. He looked at her confused. "Come. If we're correct, then they're about to trigger the last device. If what father told mother is correct, then we only have a short window of time to get to the ship. If they beat us there, then all of this will be for naught."

"Wait, I thought you said you didn't know where the ship was?" Jeffery said, confused.

Chuck smiled sadly. "How could I not know the place where my father died?"

Chapter 12

Denis stood behind the last device, his mind reeling and his heart racing. He knew that once triggered they would be only one step away from the ship. He had no idea if another tattoo would show up or if the front door of the ship would just spontaneously open up nearby. Denis knew that his time was almost up but he wasn't ready. Conrad poked Denis in the back with his gun and urged him on. Denis took a deep breath and leaned forward into the scanner, closing his eyes. He felt the tattoo dissolve and much to his excitement he felt another one immediately appear. This one was a sequence of numbers and letters that took form directly on his wrist, under the barcode. It struggled to keep form and could only pulse and fluctuate. Denis held his wrist up to the scanner where it chirped happily. A small laser appeared and burned the barcode away in flash. Denis winced but held still as the new tattoo finished taking hold. The sequence of numbers and letters glowed a bright red as they morphed into a red barcode.

Conrad took Denis by the hand, looked at the new tattoo on his wrist and cursed. "What the hell is this supposed to mean?"

Denis shrugged his shoulders and waltzed out of the room, a smile on his face. He was given another day to live.

The Major General stood with his back to the group. "We all know what must be done. It's simply a matter of when."

"As soon as he triggers the last device?" one man said.

"We need to be certain that its the last trigger before we kill him. The device requires him to not only be alive, but in relatively healthy conditions. It appears to be able to monitor his vitals." Another said.

"It has to be done before anyone finds out that he was the one to set things in motion." The Major General said and they nodded in agreement. "The world needs to think that we did this. That the power of the government is omnipotent and everlasting."

"As long as no one finds about the journals

and the research done then there's no reason to worry. As soon as changes start we isolate him until we're positive they've taken full effect. Kill him afterwards and destroy all the documentation. Tie up the loose ends." One man said and the others nodded in agreement.

"I'm glad we're all on the same page," The Major General said, "that makes this so much easier on my conscience." He pulled out a gun and proceeded to shoot everyone in the room.

Jeffery rushed into the room holding several blueprints etched on translucent paper. Chuck leapt out of her chair as Jeffery entered and cleared the table of its contents in one big swoop. Jeffery stopped, looking at the mess on the floor with surprise.

"Did you figure it out?" Chuck asked. Jeffery nodded as he lay the first sketch on the table rolling the sides out. Chuck picked up a mug from the floor and placed on a corner to hold the edge down. It was a blown up drawing of the original ship sketches from Dr. Fredrickson. Jeffery had blown the image up by hand after he had begun to decipher the blueprint notes from the journal entries. His initial difficulty had come in the fact that Charleen and Charlotte, not Charles, had written the notes and they both had been under extreme duress. When Charles had been trapped in the ship he only had a one way communication device to their home. Charles had sat day after day describing in meticulous detail what he had done in the duration of his day. Partially for records and partially out of loneliness Jeffery shook his head in disbelief. He couldn't imagine the pain of not being able to hear your loved ones voices. To be the only one able to communicate and never knowing if they actually heard you or not.

Jeffery proceeded to put layer after layer of the transparent sheets on top of the ship. Each one pertained to a specific type of modification or addition they had done to the ship over the course of twenty-five years.

As he placed the last layer on he looked up at Chuck. "Why didn't your father ever tell you what the ship did?" Jeffery asked. "Especially after he was trapped in it."

"I have always known what my role was in the activation of this ship. Before my father had gotten trapped he had treated the ship like it was this big surprise. Not only for humanity, but for me. Night after night, he would tell me about this whole new world where no one would get sick or die. Where people, like me, would be motivated by things greater than their own personal whims and fancy. That we would work collectively together to further enhance our lives. And that I was just the first step in all of that. It made the ship sound like a whimsical dream." Chuck sighed sadly. "But when he became trapped on that ship, it broke my heart. I watched it slowly kill my mother. How she couldn't handle being apart from him. Unlike her, I was engineered to be able to survive on my own if need be. I think he was afraid. That if I knew the complete truth I would not have believed in it enough to do what I had to do. That I would be consumed by my grief instead. He wanted to keep the dream alive for me."

Jeffery pulled her into a hug and squeezed her tight. They stayed like that for awhile, letting the silence comfort them.

"Okay." Jeffery said as he let her go. "Are you sure you want to know what this does then?"

Chuck nodded her head slowly. "I can no longer go into this blindly. I will still do what I have to do. But I will do it armed with the knowledge that I deserve to know."

The two of them looked at the blue print and the different layers of to it. Jeffery spread out the notes that he had translated around the blueprint. He took Chuck's hand and they studied it intently. He felt her wrist pulse as a red barcode appeared on her wrist.

"Is it time?" Jeffery asked her quietly.

Chuck nodded her head. "Do you know what it does?"

"Yeah. I think I've known for awhile, I just didn't want to believe it." Jeffery said.

Chuck squeezed his hand. "Lets go save the world." She said with a sad laugh.

As Denis boarded the plane he looked around in discomfort. The minutes were ticking by all too quickly and he hadn't been able to reach out to Jeffery. When they scanned his barcode it had spit out the current location of the famed historic Area 51. A large government conspiracy of the twentieth century. Part of him hoped that Jeffery had already figured it out. Although Denis wasn't sure how he could have. Jeffery would not only be in a personal heaven to discover that Area 51 actually existed, but to go there in person. They had rushed Denis onto the plane as soon as they had determined the coordinates. As he took his seat he saw that Jennifer had made the flight. He flashed her a quick smile before buckling in.

Denis knew that at this point, it was a matter of mere hours before they would kill him. He hoped that Conrad would be the one to do it. He'd rather die by a friends hand, even if it was an old friend who now hated his guts. He had hoped that they didn't bring Jennifer along to force her to kill him medically.

Denis pulled out yet another journal. He had found it in his room tucked under the loose floor panel. He presumed that Jeffery had it delivered to him via the informant. Most likely it was another boring diary. But anything would be better than thinking about his own death. He opened it up and by the time he had finished the first entry he had determined that it was the diary of a child, most likely a teenager. The first entry was the day that their father had died. He shuddered but continued to read on.

The child talked about duties and responsibilities. How they were responsible for nourishing and guiding their chosen mate. How they already found their mate, had produced a male heir and then got rid of their mate. How they dreaded the passing of time, waiting for their child to grow into an adult. Fearing if they had to repeat it all over again. Find their new mate, procreated and produce a male. Again and again. Denis flipped through several passages to find the entries were virtually identical. Find a new mate and have a child. Every time it was a boy. Denis counted the number of times the teenager must have mated. At least a hundred times, probably more. He was impressed. He didn't even think that he had been with that many women in his lifetime.

He closed the book, set it on his lap, and leaned back in the seat. As Denis started to drift off he found himself falling into an old dream that he hadn't had in years. He was a young child, maybe four years of age. His father held him in his arms and was very nervous. His mother on the other hand, was quite calm. She led the two of them into a dark alley; zig zagging her way thru the various vendors and shadow laced doorways. She led them down a staircase and into a small shop. She smiled at the storekeeper and took Denis out of his fathers arms. She told him to kiss daddy goodbye. He complied, not understanding the implication of her words. She handed him over to the storekeeper but his father suddenly snatched him back, clinging onto him tightly.

His parents argued over why they were even there and she reminded his father about the importance of having a barcode. That despite his lineage he still needed one in order to get by. That this was a reputable shop and Denis would have the best future money could buy. His father argued that 'they' would understand and accept their child as unique. His mother shook her head and yanked Denis from his father's arms.

"Your father tried that same line on me, as did his father and his. The one time I went along with it, they killed my son. Right in front of me. I will never let that happen again." She said defiantly as she handed Denis over to the shopkeeper.

Denis watched as the words his mother spoke sunk into his father's head. "You? You brought me here?" he said incredulously, not believing the words as they fell from his lips. "Mother?" he asked her softly with disbelief.

She kissed his father on the cheek gently. "My darling, darling boy. You were a good son and a good husband. Goodbye my love." As she stepped back two large men appeared from behind and dragged him off into the shadows. She turned back to Denis who was still in the storekeepers arms. She leaned over and kissed him on the cheek. "Now be a good boy and mommy will come find you later." She said to Denis as she tousled his hair. She looked at the store keeper and handed him several decks of cards. "Find a good family for him?" The store keeper nodded his head as Denis's mother left the shop.

The plane roughly landed with a jolt, lurching Denis out of his slumber. He was soaked with sweat, trembling, his face full of panic and fear. Jennifer was now sitting next to him, her hand on his.

"Rough landing huh?" Jennifer said, as she took notice of his state and began to check his vitals. "Are you alright?" she asked, her eyes filled with concerned.

"Just a bad dream." Denis muttered.

"You're soaked. We need to get you of these clothes and into something dry. C'mon." Jennifer said.

Denis let her lead him out of the plane and into a car. They had arrived at the infamous Area 51. Jennifer dragged Denis off into the nearest room that she could find. She stripped him out of his clothes and pushed him into a hot shower.

"I'm going to grab my medical bag. Clean up and put on some clean clothes. I'll be right back." Jennifer said before she ran off.

Denis showered quickly, probably his last shower in this lifetime he thought numbly. His mind was reeling as he wandered out into the hallway. The only thought in his head was that he had to find Jeffery. Jeffery must have figured it out. He had to be hiding somewhere on the base. When Jennifer returned she discovered that Denis had disappeared. She slung her bag over her shoulder and went off in search of him.

Denis found himself in the bowels of the base, feeling his way around in the dark, calling out for Jeffery. He was pretty sure that he was losing his mind, but he didn't care anymore. He couldn't do this alone anymore.

A door lead into yet another stairwell heading even further down. It was better lit than the rest of the building. Denis continued going further and further down the stairs into the belly o the beast.

Several floors later he opened a door and was rewarded with a brightly lit room. Denis could hear voices whispering so he carefully closed the door behind him and tiptoed his way across the room. He had only made it halfway when a hand clamped over his mouth and pulled him off into the shadows. Denis struggled briefly until he heard the familiar voice of Jeffery whispering into his ear. He turned to face his friend. They hugged and patted each other on the backs. Jeffery held him at a distance and carefully examined Denis's face.

"The tattoos are gone?" Jeffery asked him.

Denis shook his head and showed him the red barcode on his right wrist. Jeffery laughed.

"What's so funny?" Denis asked.

"I'll tell you later. We have much to discuss and not enough time." Jeffery stated.

"I know, I have so many things I need to share with you too." Denis said in a rush. "My mother. I remember her now." He exclaimed.

Jeffery abruptly hugged Denis again. "I am

so sorry that I never believed you before."
Jeffery said. "Forgive me."

Denis looked at him shocked. "You know?"

Jeffery nodded. "Chuck told me. It was, uh, a
bit distressing at first. Difficult to digest."

"Tell me about it." Denis said rolling his eyes.
"Wait. How does Chuck know?"

"We-ll. That is an interesting story in itself."
Jeffery started.

"Denis. We know you're down here. Stop
hiding in the shadows already." Conrad shouted
from above.

Jeffery and Denis glanced at each other.

"I'll find you." Jeffery insisted, disappearing
into the shadows.

Conrad shined a light on Denis's face. "There
you are. Come back upstairs already. The
doctor has been storming about like a mad
woman worried over you." Conrad said,
hauling Denis across the room. "What the hell
are you doing down here?"

"Chasing shadows." Denis said absently.

Denis sat on a bed as Jennifer was checking his
vitals. "I'm sorry if I frightened you earlier." He
said, wrapping his arms around her waist and
pulling her in for a kiss.

Jennifer kissed him back gently and then
pushed herself away. "Don't ever do that again.

Or these," she said indicating her lips, "will no longer be valid medical treatment for you."

"Oooh, I like a woman who's sassy." Denis said as he cupped her buttocks and pulled her up onto the bed with him. "Help me doctor. I have this body part that keeps getting hard and I don't know what to do about it."

Jennifer laughed and leaned in to kiss him. Denis wrapped his arms around her as they embraced deeply. The sound of someone clearing their throat broke apart their kiss. Jennifer nimbly slid down off the bed landing softly on the floor. She tidied her dress, brushing her hair smooth at the same time. Denis sat up straight, looking over Jennifer's shoulders to see a young solider standing in the doorway.

"They're waiting for you in the conference room Mr. Roy." The solider said, embarrassed at his intrusion.

"Thank you solider, dismissed." Denis said and the solider scurried off. Denis stood up and kissed Jennifer again. He went towards the door, looked back at her with a smile then left.

Jennifer rushed out of the room as soon as Denis disappeared around the corner. She ran for the nearest stairwell and made her way down to the twenty fifth floor. Just before Denis had returned a solider had dropped off a package of medical supplies. Inside she found a box filled with empty syringes. A note had been inserted inside one of them. Knowing that time was incredibly precious she ran down the stairs at full speed, not noticing that she was being followed.

As she entered the twenty fifth floor a hand caught the door before it could close behind her. Conrad waited patiently, until he was sure that Jennifer was out of audible range and slipped in silently behind her. As Conrad made his way across the room he could see that Jennifer talking to someone. Conrad watched her eyes grow wide with surprise and he wondered what she knew and whether or not it was worth knowing. Probably not, Conrad thought to himself. He crept closer until he could who she was talking too. Conrad was surprised to see Jeffery. He had ordered Jeffery's death himself. Now Conrad had to kill them both himself.

Jeffery handed Jennifer a piece of paper and she looked it over quickly, her face filling with awe. She quickly hugged Jeffery before he disappeared back into the shadows. Once she was certain that Jeffery was gone Jennifer headed back towards the stairwell. As she rounded the corner she ran smack dab into Conrad.

"Conrad. Hi. What are you doing here?" Jennifer asked him, visibly flustered.

"I could ask you the same thing. Or perhaps you can just tell your father yourself. That the mole I've been searching for is you." Conrad said as a sinister grin grew across his face.

Jennifer took a step back and then another.

"Go ahead. I love the chase." Conrad chuckled.

Jennifer took off running. Conrad pursued and quickly caught up with her. He grabbed her by the hair and slammed her face into the wall.

"Stupid Jennifer." Conrad said as pushed her towards the floor.

Dazed Jennifer back-pedalled away from Conrad and slipped in her own blood. Conrad reached down, grabbed her shirt and pulled her towards him. He blew her a kiss then head butted her. She flew backwards and rolled along the floor.

"Is Denis worth dying for? Really? That dumbass?" Conrad said as he crouched down beside her. He grabbed Jennifer by the hair and lifted her head off of the ground. "If you had just been a good girl and followed orders you could have stayed by my side."

Jennifer spit a gob of saliva and blood into his face. "He's better in bed then you'll ever be." She said smugly and Conrad punched her in the face.

He screamed in an furious rage as he stood up and began kicking Jennifer repeatedly in the stomach. When he felt his anger begin to subside he stormed off cursing both her and Denis.

Denis ran back into the med bay. "False alarm, no one was there. Shall we pick up where we left —" his voice trailed off as he saw the med bay was empty. He laid down on the bed and decided to wait for her. She couldn't have gone far. He felt something poking his back and found a crumpled up piece of paper. It was the note Jeffery had addressed to Jennifer. It told her to go to the twenty fifth floor as quickly as possible. Denis got to his feet and flew down the hallway.

As he entered the twenty fifth floor Denis called out to Jennifer and Jeffery. He had made his way halfway across the dark room when he saw a body lying on the floor surrounded in blood. Denis called Jennifer's name frantically as he ran over and knelt down beside her. He grabbed Jennifer under the shoulders, his arm cradling her head, the other shaking her gently.

"Jennifer, Jennifer. Can you hear me? Wake up. Please wake up." Denis cried out.

Her eyelids fluttered softly. "Denis?" Jennifer

said weakly.

Denis grabbed her left hand and kissed it, stroking his cheek with it. "Who did this to you? Jeffery?"

"Con—con—ra—" Jennifer said, her voice trailing off.

"No, no ,no. Hold on Jennifer. You can do this. I can take you upstairs. We'll fix you up, okay?"

"Denis. Stop." Jennifer said, her voice weak yet firm. "I need — tell you— portant."

"Hush baby. Save your energy." Denis pleaded with her, caressing her face with his hand.

"Doesn't save us. Kills us."

"What are you talking about? Don't talk crazy. Everything is going to be okay."

Jennifer reached her left hand up towards his face. It shook badly until Denis grabbed it. "Take it." She said as she opened her hand in his.

Inside her hand was a crumpled up photograph. He tried to flatten it as best he could. On it was a set of twins, twenty or so and a teenaged girl that looked a lot like his mother.

"Where did you get this?" Denis asked her. He turned it over, on the back an inscription was scrawled *"Mother, Father and Charlotte"*. Only Charlotte had been scratched out and *"Chuck"* was scribbled over it. It was impossible. He flipped the photograph back over. They were twins and the younger girl barely a few years younger than them. They were all basically the same age as their daughter and she was a dead ringer for his mother.

Jennifer's hand fell out of his and landed limply on the ground beside her body. Denis looked down at Jennifer and roared. He pulled her close to him, tears flowing freely and cried out in anger.

Chapter 13

Back on the main floor of the base Denis stormed through the halls, slamming doors as he went. He was covered in Jennifers blood, the picture still clenched tightly in his fist and a fierce look on his face. His nostrils flared and his eyes burned for revenge. Conrad came out of a nearby room and Denis raced down the hall towards him, screaming as he did. Denis slammed Conrad up against the wall, pinning him by the throat with his forearm. He began punching Conrad repeatedly in the face.

It took several men and several punches to pry Denis off of Conrad. When they had succeeded Conrad fell to the ground, his knees buckling beneath him as he gasped, air hissing in thru his teeth.

"Why did you do it?" Denis screamed at Conrad.

"Sedate him." Conrad ordered. "But keep him conscious."

One of the soldiers reached down to help him to his feet but Conrad slapped his hand away. He mumbled something about being fine while demanding an ice pack. By the time Conrad got to his feet, had an ice pack on his cheek and had stumbled his way over to Denis the sedative had begun to take effect. Denis struggled to free himself but they easily held him down. Conrad held the ice pack to the side with his left hand and with his right hand, punched Denis squarely in the face.

"Take him downstairs and prep him for the final stage." Conrad barked as he limped away.

Denis sat with his newly appointed guards on either side of him, admist a pile of rubble a few kilometres away from the base and approximately five kilometres underground. His hands were tied together in front and he held a bag of ice on his cheek. Conrad, with clumsily done fresh stitches on his nose, and the Major General joined him.

"Where are we going?" Denis asked, "Disneyland?"

Ignoring Denis, the Major General gave a nod and Conrad took the lead. Denis was pulled to his feet and led down an old corridor. A previous explosion had taken out several of the floors above. Aside from scorch marks the floor seemed relatively and surprisingly undamaged. Conrad led them thru a maze of broken walls, strewn about electrical cables and dangling bits of rebar. After what seemed like hours they finally stopped in front of a large metal door. To the right of the door was a black plexiglass like panel. A non portable scanner of sorts.

Conrad nodded at the soldiers holding Denis and they dragged him to the panel. They pulled his sleeve up to reveal the still vibrant red barcode and pressed it against the scanner. It came to life and chirped. The sound of air hissing escaped from the door as it creaked and groaned before slowing sliding open. Conrad stepped in first, then the Major General, followed by Denis and his entourage. One soldier yanking Denis by the forearm while the other poking a gun into his back.

Denis paused long enough to take in the enormity of what lay before them. They were on a circular stairwell in a large empty hall like room that vaguely resembled the interior of a launching bay. Denis leaned over the railing and could see that far down below them was the top of a ship. A spaceship. A real life, honest to goodness spaceship. Denis laughed knowing that Jeffery had been right all along. The soldier yanked on his arm and they continued down the staircase in silence.

As they progressed down the staircase the initially barren space became further occupied with the ship. The exterior walls were a dull grey and a mottled brown. The colours fluctuated as if they were alive and breathing. Denis could feel his wrist twitch as they approached the ship. Standing beside it the barcode was practically humming to Denis. The entire exterior shell appeared to be seamless and there were no openings of any kind. Further down, the staircase turned into a catwalk that stretched out along one side of the ship. They continued down the catwalk until it ended roughly at the ships midway mark. Looking around they saw nothing. No seams, no doors, no windows, no openings of any kind. No way in.

Conrad turned to face Denis. "Open it." He ordered and the soldiers pushed Denis forward, pressing him up against the ship. Denis held his still tied up hands above his head and shrugged his shoulders. Conrad shook his head and pushed Denis back against the ship.

"I don't know what to —" Denis started and he stopped as he heard the sound of a gun being cocked at the side of his head. "I'll figure it out." He squeaked. He began to wave his wrist about, hoping it would activate a door of some kind or if the ship was intelligent it would magically suck him inside and leave the rest of them out on the catwalk. When nothing happened Denis turned slowly to face Conrad, a pleading look on his face. Suddenly he felt a draft of air hit him from behind.

"Jeffery?" Conrad said, puzzled. He moved his gun from Denis's head and aimed it past him, at Jeffery. Denis reached up with his arms and knocked the gun out of Conrad's hand. The gun went flying upwards, bounced off of the outer hull of the ship, clattered back onto the catwalk and slipped through the grate and down into the never ending abyss below. They all paused, waiting to hear the clatter of the gun hitting the ground below them. Only it never did.

Denis felt himself get tugged backwards and he turned to see Jeffery standing in a hole in the exterior of the ship. Without exchanging a single word the two of them took off quickly into the ship with the others in hot pursuit. Conrad screamed, ordering the soldiers to capture them both. Dead or alive. Jeffery nimbly ducked thru several corridors, like he had lived there his whole life. He pulled Denis into a small nook and they stood silent as the soldiers ran past. Jeffery looked over Denis's shoulder and motioned that the coast was clear. They ran down a few more corridors until Jeffery pulled Denis into a small room.

After confirming that they were alone Denis turned to face Jeffery, holding his hands up. Jeffery untied the rope.

"How the hell did you get on this ship?" Denis asked.

"Chuck let me in." Jeffery answered.

"Chuck let you in," Denis started, as he pulled the bloodied photo he had gotten from Jennifer out of his pocket. "This Chuck?" He finished and Jeffery nodded. "The same Chuck, a guy, that looks just like my mother?" Denis asked.

"Is your mother." Jeffery corrected him. "And your grandmother, and your great grandmother and so on. Wow. That sounds even more disturbing out loud than it did in my head."

"What?" Denis said, confused as hell.

Jeffery slapped a hand over Denis's mouth and pressed up against the wall. They heard the sound of footsteps approaching the room. They stopped outside it and then continue on down the corridor.

"We have to get to the main control unit. But there's something I need to tell you first." Jeffery said.

"Can it wait until after we save the world?" Denis asked, urging him to lead the way.

"Not really." Jeffery said and they both fell silent again as they heard footsteps again. This time they came into the room. The two of them were pressed up tight against the wall, partially hidden by a large purple plant. They remained motionless as Conrad continued further into the room. The two of them snuck past the plant and darted out into the corridor. As they broke off into a run they could hear Conrad calling out after them.

"Shit, he saw us." Denis said as he looked over his shoulder to see Conrad run out of the room behind them.

"This way." Jeffery instructed taking a sharp turn to the right. Denis followed and they clambered down a set of stairs. Conrad let off a few shots that ricocheted above them.

"Keep moving." Denis hollered as they ducked under ducting. Jeffery was leading them through the ships inner bowels.

"The blood," Jeffery started, "on the picture."

"Don't ask." Denis said, his voice growing tense.

Jeffery sighed softly and indicated that Denis stand in the corner. Jeffery hid behind a large vent.

Denis looked at him bewildered. "You're just

going to leave me out in the open?"

"Trust me." Jeffery said as he knelt down low.

Conrad came bursting around the corner and saw Denis with his back to the wall. Conrad laughed, holding the gun out in front of him. "Aww, you're taking all the fun out of it." He said menacingly as he continued to step towards Denis.

Denis looked at Conrad then snuck a glance at Jeffery. He plastered a fake smile on his face. Holding his hands up high Denis went to take a step forward. Jeffery hissed at him and Denis immediately stopped in his tracks. Conrad turned to see where the noise had come from but didn't see anything. He turned his attention back to Denis who had backed up even further into the corner. When Conrad was almost within arms reach he heard Jeffery grunt loudly. Conrad turned and fired off a shot wildly in his direction. Seconds later the ground beneath Conrad disappeared and he fell into the pit below.

Denis looked down to see Conrad, his arm most likely broken, laying on the ground several feet below them unconscious. He hopped over the hole and went over to Jeffery. Denis held his hand out, "You can come out, he's gone." As he knelt down he saw that Jeffery wasn't moving. "Oh shit." He said pulling Jeffery out from underneath the vent.

Jeffery moaned, clutching his stomach. "Just a flesh wound. I'll be fine."

Denis ripped a section of his shirt off, lifted Jeffery's hand and place the fabric underneath. "Hold it down tight. Lets get you upright and find this control station." As Denis tried to pull Jeffery to his feet he protested loudly to be put back down. They both collapsed to the ground.

"You can find the control station on your own. Its in the centre of the ship. Find Chuck, she'll help you save the world." Jeffery said as he coughed loudly, literally hacking his lungs into his hand.

"If I leave you here, you're going to die." Denis said.

"We're all going to die anyway once you activate the ship." Jeffery said, coughing again.

"What are you talking about?" Denis said softly. "The ship is supposed to save humanity, not destroy it."

"Sometimes you need to break a few eggs to make an omelet." Jeffery coughed.

Denis shook his head. "If its going to destroy us, then I won't activate it."

"You need to do the right thing. The worst you can do now is nothing." Jeffery mumbled, his voice growing weak.

"Tell me what to do Jeffery." Denis pleaded.

"Save us Denis. From ourselves." Jeffery said as he coughed once last time. Denis closed his friends eyes and lay him gently down on the grate, a lump forming in his throat, tears curling at the corners of his eyes.

Denis got to his feet and held his barcode up in front of him. "Now would be a good time to be helpful." He yelled out to the ship as he waved his wrist in the air. As he waved it over the catwalk to his left he felt it begin to tingle. He laughed and took off down the catwalk.

Denis ran thru the open door and found himself in a mammoth room. It was immensely bright and open. The walls were made of small cubicle like drawers. He felt his barcode pulse excitedly. Below him on the lower level in the centre of the floor was an oversized console. He saw a ladder, grabbed the outer rails with his hands, whipped his feet to outside of the rails and slid down. Denis landed on the ground hard, fell backwards and rolled halfway across the floor. He groaned but laughed, clutching his side.

"It's about time. I was starting to think that you had chickened out."

Denis got to his feet and saw Chuck. She wore shorts with a wide oversized orange belt that hung snugly over her hips, a tight black tank top and a midriff cropped army cargo jacket. On her head was an oversized pageboy hat. Chuck pulled the hat off and long blonde hair cascaded down, going well past her waist.

Unable to process what he was seeing Denis could only mumble 'Mom?' incoherently.

Chuck smiled at Denis. "Hi sweetie. How have you been?" she asked sarcastically.

"I've been better? You?" Denis said slowly, approaching her and the console.

"I'm sorry that I've been away from you for so long." Chuck said carefully.

"That's okay. I'm not sure how comfortable I would have been procreating with my own mother, so its cool." Denis said awkwardly.

"There's so much that I want to tell you." Chuck said, unsure of where and how to start.

"How about with, why are you here?" Denis asked.

"Because it takes two to tango, doesn't it?" the Major General said as he entered the room with the two soldiers close behind him, his gun trained on Chuck.

Denis looked from the Major General to Chuck. "What does he mean?"

"That it takes two of you to activate the ship." The Major General stated. "And I will be the other one, sorry son, no hard feelings." He said as he fired a shot off, catching Denis in the shoulder. Chuck screamed as Denis collapsed to the ground. He clutched his shoulder, blood rapidly oozing out between his fingers. The Major General trained his gun on Chuck and ordered her back to the console.

"Don't do this. It needs to be pure. You lack my DNA." Chuck cried out.

"Oh don't feed me that bullshit. It only needs to be a descendant to activate the ship." The Major General said smugly.

"If that's true, then why did your twin sister die when trying to trigger the device?" Chuck said firmly.

The Major General's face grew dark. His eyes flickered with anger as he turned his attention towards Denis who lay on the floor in a growing pool of blood. "Because the devices were designed to be trigger by male DNA. She," he said pointing towards Chuck, "procreated with Dr. Fredrickson's son and produced another male heir. Dr. Fredrickson had manipulated his son's DNA so that whenever his descendant and Charlotte mated, a male would be produced. If the tattoo didn't manifest on the boy by his twenty-fifth birthday, Charolette would mate with her son, bear another and then kill the 'older' of the two sons, her current husband. Then she handed her younger son over to a group sworn to protect the lineage so the child would be 'assigned' a programmable barcode.

Then she would come back when he had grown up to see if he bore the 'miraculous' tattoo."

"How do you know all of this?" Denis asked, pulling himself up against the wall. Fighting to not slump back down.

"Charlotte." the Major General said smugly.

Chuck glared at the Major General before turning to face Denis. "Sometimes, the barcodes inked on my children accidentally allowed them to mate with someone else. Programming the barcodes is not foolproof. When that happens, a daughter is usually produced."

"And?" Denis asked, almost afraid of the answer he would hear.

"I'd have to kill his family."

Denis looked at her horrified. The Major General roared with laughter.

"You have to keep the gene pool clean, no cross contamination, isn't that right Charlotte?"

Chuck glared at the Major General. "He had to mate with me or the mission would be over. If I mated with an offspring not descended from myself then it could take centuries to wash out the bad DNA."

Denis stared in shock at Chuck. The Major General punch Denis in the face knocking him over.

Denis rolled over onto his back and moaned in pain. "How the hell did she let an ass like you live?"

The Major General knelt down beside Denis and pressed a finger into his gunshot wound. "Because my father mated with a normal human and had twins. One boy and one girl. Charlotte didn't know what to do. She watched from afar as we both grew up. The tattoo, however, manifested on my sister. Not me. Since I was already in the military my sister was assigned to me. Charlotte approached us and explained enough about this," he said, waving his hand up in the air at the immense room above him, "to not only peak my interest but to sacrifice my sister. When my sister died at the first console I let Charlotte go. I let her think that she had gotten away scott free. I then focused my energies on attempting to trigger the tattoo on myself. I never expected them to manifest on someone else within my lifetime." He roared with laughter. "And here I am. About to become king of my very own castle."

The Major General grabbed Charlotte and pulled her closer to him. He walked her over towards the console, the gun trained on her head. "Kill him." He ordered and the soldiers jumped to life, quickly approaching Denis.

Chuck screamed out as the Major General dragged her towards the console. He grabbed her by the arm and yanked. She fought him, punching, kicking and biting him. "You're going to get us all killed." She cried out.

They pulled Denis to his feet and went to punch him in the face when out of nowhere Conrad yelled out. "He's mine." firing a shot wildly into the air. One of the soldiers face exploded, his body crumpling to the ground. "Shit." Conrad said as he came around the corner. His right arm was badly bent and hanging limply from its socket. He held his gun in his left hand. "Can't aim worth shit with this hand. Stand still will you mate." He said as he fired off another shot towards Denis.

Denis dove to the ground as the other soldier fell beside him. He wasn't dead, but he certainly was going to wish he was. Denis crawled along the floor as Conrad continue to fire shots wildly. Just as Denis was pressed up against the wall and Conrad was mere feet away another gun fired. Blood bloomed on Conrad's chest and spread out onto his shirt. His gun slid from his fingers onto the ground at Denis's feet. Conrad clutched at his chest as he fell to his knees. Blood gurgled out of his mouth as he fell down, dead before he even hit the ground.

The Major General sighed heavily. "I'm quite tired of all these interruptions." He said pointing his gun towards Denis and firing. It clicked with the sound of an empty chamber and as it did Chuck cried out, pulling a knife out of her shirt and stabbing the Major General in his abdomen. He turned towards her, grabbed her by the neck and started choking her. Denis grabbed the gun at his feet, drew it steady and fired. The Major General looked at Denis irritated, let go of Chuck and clutched at the hole in his throat. He stumbled backwards, tripped over Conrad and fell onto the ground.

Denis pulled himself to his feet and Chuck rushed over to help steady him. Together they made their way to the console. She entered in a sequence of commands and two holes opened up.

"We're really doing this aren't we?" Denis said, unsure if he should laugh or not.

"I made a promise, a long time ago." Chuck said.

They stood at the console in silence.

"We're going to die, aren't we." Denis said. More a rhetoric statement than a question.

"If Jeffery, is indeed correct, then this ship will terraform the entire planet." Chuck said softly. "So, yeah. We're probably going to die."

"You know. Of all the ways that I imagined myself dying. Dying with my own mother while saving all of humanity was never on the list." Denis said with a laugh.

"I could have been your wife instead." Chuck

said, a sly smile on her lips.

"Ewww, gross. Way to ruin the moment mom." Denis said stepping away from the console and looking at her with utter repugnance.

Chuck took Denis's hand and squeezed it tightly. "I never got to tell any of my sons this before, but I'm very proud of you."

Denis looked at Chuck, the love in her eyes surpassed only by the loneliness in them. He squeezed her hand back. "Lets do this."

They turned to face the console together. Two holes appeared in the terminal in front of them. Still holding hands they each held a free hand above the holes. Together they lowered their hands, wincing as it grabbed them and held them firmly in place. The ship suddenly came to life and churned loudly as the engines began to initiate. Denis turned to face Chuck, pulled her hand to his face and kissed it gently. He drew her in close, letting go of her hand and putting his arm around her shoulders. He closed his eyes and leaned his head atop of hers as a single tear slid down his cheek.